Georgetown Interiors
Alison Sherwood

Blake rose abruptly, the business card curled lightly in his hand, and paced the length of his office, thinking about the woman he'd met in Valentino's, the hardly respectable lingerie store his firm had just acquired in a package deal.

He paused and pondered the coincidence of the tempestuous encounter with Ms. Sherwood. In her flight from the shop she'd dropped her business card, revealing her true identity.

He'd been looking for a new design firm to handle his contracts, and he had a feeling Ms. Sherwood was more than qualified. She had an intense effect on him, and it didn't revolve solely around design.

Idly he wondered what was hidden beneath her voluminous red cape. But more puzzling, what would a successful Washington designer be doing in a place like Valentino's? Sight-seeing? A wicked grin stole over his face at the thought of their *future* encounter, and her reaction to the decorating job he had in mind....

Dear Reader,

Welcome to Silhouette—experience the magic of the wonderful world where two people fall in love. Meet heroines that will make you cheer for their happiness, and heroes (be they the boy next door or a handsome, mysterious stranger) who will win your heart. Silhouette Romance reflects the magic of love—sweeping you away with books that will make you laugh and cry, heartwarming, poignant stories that will move you time and time again.

In the coming months we're publishing romances by many of your all-time favorites, such as Diana Palmer, Brittany Young, Sondra Stanford and Annette Broadrick. Your response to these authors and our other Silhouette Romance authors has served as a touchstone for us, and we're pleased to bring you more books with Silhouette's distinctive medley of charm, wit and—above all—*romance*.

I hope you enjoy this book and the many stories to come. Experience the magic!

Sincerely,

Tara Hughes
Senior Editor
Silhouette Books

LYDIA LEE

Valentino's Pleasure

Silhouette *Romance*

Published by Silhouette Books New York

America's Publisher of Contemporary Romance

For my sister, Anne Weeks Hancock,
and my brother, Joseph Preble Weeks,
with love and gratitude.

Special thanks:
To my mother, Caroline, for all her reading.
To my good friend Michael Rossoff
for helping me keep balance.
To the Washington Romance Writers
for their support.

SILHOUETTE BOOKS
300 E. 42nd St., New York, N.Y. 10017

Copyright © 1989 by Lydia Lee

ISBN: 0-373-08642-3

First Silhouette Books printing April 1989

Printed in the U.S.A.

LYDIA LEE

lives near Washington, D.C., where she was born and raised. From an early age it was her lifetime dream to be both an actress and a published author. Her theatrical goal was achieved at the Dallas Theatre Center, where, as actress, playwright and designer, she received the coveted Greer Garson Theatre Arts Award. In time, however, she discovered that only writing could fulfill her creative desires. After returning east several years ago, she dedicated herself to this, and hasn't stopped since. When not writing, she enjoys reading, traveling and the company of friends. Lydia describes herself as an incurable romantic who believes in dreams, magic and happy endings. She has also published under the name Rose Marie Lima.

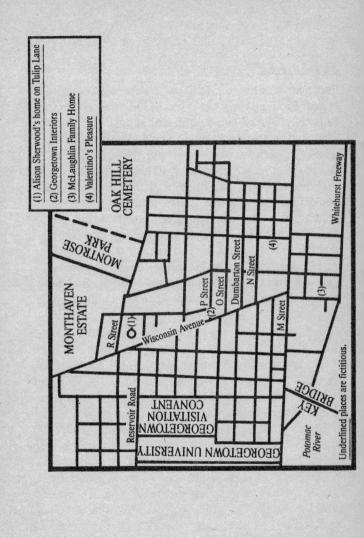

(1) Alison Sherwood's home on Tulip Lane
(2) Georgetown Interiors
(3) McLaughlin Family Home
(4) Valentino's Pleasure

OAK HILL CEMETERY

MONTROSE PARK

MONTHAVEN ESTATE

R Street
Wisconsin Avenue
P Street
O Street
Dumbarton Street
N Street
M Street

Whitehurst Freeway

Reservoir Road

GEORGETOWN VISITATION CONVENT

GEORGETOWN UNIVERSITY

KEY BRIDGE

Potomac River

Underlined places are fictitious.

Chapter One

All our girls have special names," the manager, an enormous creature in pink sequins, murmured as her heavily made-up eyes flicked over the length of Alison Sherwood's body. 'We'll call you 'Cotton Candi'!'' Thrusting a frothy piece of something decidedly indecent and a pair of fishnet stockings at Alison, she pointed out the dressing room. "After you've changed, I'd like you to relieve Bubbles on the red swing." The manager offered an incandescent smile and added, "My name's Pink Glitter. Don't worry about a thing, you'll catch on quick!"

Alison took a deep breath to steady herself and in measured tones said, "There's been some mistake."

"You don't like the night shift?" Pink Glitter leaned against the counter and blew smoke rings. A fog of smoke circled her pink-and-gold spiked hair. Alison blinked dumbfounded at this study in glitter, every inch of the other woman spangled with gold. A pearl stud was implanted with a vengeance in the side of Pink Glitter's nose.

God help her if she ever got a cold. She was clutching her cigarette holder with the studied air reminiscent of Gloria Swanson in *Sunset Boulevard*, waiting for a reply.

"No!" Alison managed to blurt out. "Not the night, or the day shift!"

"Well, when the hell do you wanna work, honey? Because for once, the agency sent me exactly what I asked for." Snuffing out her cigarette, she added. "A little class, Cotton Candi, 'cause you'd be surprised at some of our clients."

"Nothing would surprise me," Alison said through clenched teeth. "And my name's not Cotton Candi, and furthermore, I did not come here to sit in your red swing!"

"You mean you're a customer?" Pink Glitter's mouth dropped open at the possibility. "But you look just like what I asked for: tall, slim...and that old-fashioned hairdo...." She gestured vaguely to Alison's topknot as if it were the definitive piece of identification.

"I am not a customer!" Alison heard herself shout. She, Alison O'Shaunnessey Sherwood, hardworking, down-to-earth mother of three had just been mistaken for a customer—even worse, a salesclerk—in a place called Valentino's Pleasure.

"Hey, keep it down! Our new owner is right over there."

"Oh, he is, is he?" Alison's eyes narrowed. Her gaze swept across racks of intimate attire that shimmered under black light. She spotted the new owner staring at her with something akin to amusement. As far as Alison was concerned, there was not one ounce of humor to be wrung from being mistaken for a salesgirl in this sleazy establishment. There was something definitely shady about the place, as if illicit deals went on in back rooms. Alison's imagination took flight, and with an expression of grim determination she briskly strode in the owner's direction.

"You're the owner of this..." She choked on the word, which the man neatly supplied.

"Sex shop?" Amusement curved sensuous lips. "You have something against...sex shops?" An unaccustomed wave of heat suffused Alison's face as his dark gaze swept over her in obvious approval. Looking into her eyes, he queried softly, "Cotton Candi, is it?"

"It is not! Whatever fragment of conversation you overheard, you're as mistaken as—" with an impatient wave of her hand she indicated the manager "—as Pink Glitter. But you," she continued in a hardened voice, "you're the cause of half the problems in this country! Don't you realize it's places like this that are breeding grounds for vice and corruption? Hiding behind a three-piece suit doesn't spell respectability." Alison heard her voice steadily climb in a futile effort to drown out the Rolling Stones singing "I can't get no satisfaction." Bubbles had slipped off her red satin perch and, along with other denizens of the evening, had flocked around the oddly matched duo. The air was heavy with perfume and greasepaint.

Pink Glitter took the role of referee. "You can't go talking to our new owner like that," she bleated, intimating he was practically their leader. She shook her head with such vigor that Alison was certain porcupine quills would fly.

"I can, and I am."

The man with the dark eyes affirmed it. "You most certainly are. However, I feel I should say something in my defense." He quirked a smile at the glittery manager, adding, "You and the other girls can go back to business. I'll handle this customer's complaint."

"For the final time, I am *not* a customer!"

"Promise?" he teased. There was a sparkling light in his ebony eyes as he pressed on. "You know, you have it all wrong about me."

"Oh?" she managed, despite the fact her heart did a curious flip-flop. "I suppose this newly acquired business donates its money to charity? Please, I wasn't born yesterday. If there was ever a joint, this is it." A dramatic sweep of her hand encompassed the throbbing Valentino's Pleasure with its floor-to-ceiling mirrors and fluorescent airport runway aisles. "Just look at the place! You could go blind, deaf and catch God-knows-what walking in the door!"

"I agree," he replied with unexpected candor.

"You do?" She blinked back at him and took a deep breath as the music subsided.

"I do. As for looking at Valentino's, that's exactly what I was doing when you descended upon me with your...opinion." His lips eased into a smile, and Alison found herself staring at him. The three-piece suit she had made scathing reference to was obviously tailor-made. Its charcoal-colored wool heightened his dark eyes and salt-and-pepper hair. This man had a magnetic appeal that even Alison in her temper couldn't miss. She stood immobile, gazing into velvet-black eyes that crinkled with amusement.

"As I said, I couldn't agree with you more."

"But you're the new owner," Alison protested, stirring herself to some of her former indignation.

"Yes. My company bought out Computease Amalgamated, and Valentino's turned out to be part of the deal. I was in New Orleans and wanted to see what the main store looked like." With a weary shrug he added, "We'll be selling the entire chain."

"There's more than one?"

"Key West, Chicago, San Francisco, New Orleans and Washington, D.C.," he recited wearily. "And they'll be somebody else's baby after next week." He smiled. "So you see, I'm not into white slavery *or* high kink, after all."

"Well, I...that is—" Alison swallowed. Fumbling in her bag, she reached for the keys to her rented car. She was painfully aware of having just made a complete fool of herself and, flushed with mortification, wanted to get out with as much dignity as possible.

"You never did say why *you* were here?" he prodded.

"It was all a mistake," she heard herself mutter as she backed into a rack of black satin garter belts. Brushing back her hair from her face, she edged nearer the door and pulled her red wool cape around her as if it might render her invisible. "Just a mistake," she repeated, and, hurrying past the pink neon flamingos that flanked the fluorescent aisle, she made her way onto crowded Bourbon Street. She paused once to look back at Valentino's. Bubbles was again perched high on the red satin swing, her backside on prominent display in the front window. There was no way Alison's sister, Sarah, would work in such a place. Was there?

Alison had come down to New Orleans to attend a designers' conference and had taken the opportunity to look in on her sister, only to discover she had moved with no forwarding address. Her last letter had mentioned a fabulous new and different job at Valentino's. Obviously there was another place by the same name. Ten years and several galaxies separated the sisters. Both were creative and both had quick tempers, but the the similarities stopped there. Alison, a thirty-eight-year-old widow with three children, had carved a successful niche for herself as an interior designer. Sarah, single, dabbled in the arts and theater, and considered life to be one long banquet—all hors d'oeuvres. She had tried a main course of marriage to a banker whose preferences didn't include her. Two years later Sarah got a settlement and at twenty-four began to find herself. Alison knew her sister had packed a lot of living into those years, but dangling from a swing on Bourbon Street was too much even for Sarah. Alison was confident she would find her, enjoy a catch-up visit and return to the sanity of her cozy home in Georgetown.

Blake McLaughlin swiveled in his chair. From behind his expensive mahogany desk he could stare out the plate-glass window to the street twenty stories below. People scurried like ants in the freshly falling snow, and Wilson Boulevard traffic was already backing up. Key Bridge would be a mess going home. Turning to his desk, he pushed the intercom button. "I want four copies of the new holdings report, and send one by telex to Chicago. Special notifications on the VP contract. Tell Lew I've decided not to sell, and that something's in the works." At the murmured assent on the other end of the line, Blake glanced once again at the business card in front of him that read Georgetown Interiors—Alison Sherwood. Cotton Candi, he thought as he rose abruptly, the card curled lightly in his hand. Pacing the length of his office, he thought about the woman he'd met in Valentino's. He paused midstride, inches from the window. His breath frosted the view as he pondered the coincidence of their tempestuous encounter. In her flight from the sex shop, her business card had dropped, revealing not only her true identity, but the fact that she was practically a neighbor—*and* in a profession that gave Blake McLaughlin pause to reconsider Valentino's fate. He'd been looking for a new design firm to handle their contracts, and he had a feeling Ms. Sherwood was more than qualified.

Upon Blake's return home, he'd contacted Georgetown Interiors and requested an appointment with Ms. Sherwood. A wicked grin stole over his face at the thought of their *future* encounter and her reaction to the decorating job he had in mind. She had quite a temper. He guessed her to be about thirty, maybe younger. It was hard to tell exactly. She'd had an intense effect on him that didn't revolve solely around design. Idly he wondered what was hidden beneath that voluminous red cape. But more puzzling, what would a successful Washington designer be doing in Valentino's? Sight-seeing?

He gazed again at her card, ecru colored with a trompe l'oeil border in rich burgundy that matched the raised lettering. Elegant, dynamic, very like Ms. Sherwood. Though their meeting had been brief, he was thoroughly intrigued by her. It was crazy, but he'd been fantasizing about her since returning home. No woman had affected him quite like this, not since his wife, Ginny, who had died three years ago. That first year following her death was still shrouded in a painful haze. That someone as lovely and vivacious as Ginny should suddenly die had practically devastated him. Only his work had kept him from going mad. After the initial shock wore off, he began dating other women, though he always compared them to his deceased wife. Granted, they were beautiful women and enjoyed the fact that he was rich, powerful and knew the Right People. The trappings were a joke to him, but they kept the right doors open, so who was he to argue?

Growing up dirt-poor in a small Texas town meant he knew what it was like to go without. He'd left home at fifteen and begun his real education on the streets. When he was twenty-two he used his knowledge, natural abilities and a streak of genius to make himself indispensable to a fledgling computer company. A single unique invention gave him the necessary bankroll to invest in real estate. In five years he went to the top of his own private mountain, named it Camelot Enterprises, and now *he* issued the tickets and called the shots. No one had gotten the better of him. As a charming eligible widower, attractive women were constantly pursuing him. So why did he have this obsession with a woman he didn't know? It puzzled him.

Glancing out the window once again and seeing the rapidly falling snow, he remembered the weather report called for three inches changing to icy rain around midnight.

The intercom crackled to life, announcing Lew Mathieson on line one. Blake snapped forward in his leather chair and punched the extension.

"The stats are on the way," Blake said without preamble. "And I've decided to hold on to Valentino's and do a total revamp."

"What made you change your mind?" the voice on the other end of the line asked. "Just yesterday you said 'sell!'"

"That was yesterday. I've been mulling it over. Why not use the name and give it some class?"

"Class? You said it was campy and kinky. Not exactly what Camelot would go for, though the chain's doing one hell of a business."

"And will continue to, but not in their present form," Blake replied. "The French Quarter's becoming very popular with young professionals. A different type of Valentino's could do very well there; likewise the one in Georgetown. We'll want to check out the other locations."

"Right. We don't want anything to reflect back on Camelot." Lew laughed uneasily.

"You're damn straight we don't. Computease Amalgamated is probably the biggest acquisition we've got yet. I was looking over the list: Video chains, Artex Gas Stations, Farmacon Dairy, Hallmark Hotels, not to mention the lucrative Valentino's." He rattled the names off like gunfire. "So tender those papers carefully, counselor."

"Like my own children, Blake. Speaking of kids, how are Willy and Sondra?"

Blake paused and let out a sigh, "Sondra's the same, and Willy's still playing that infernal trumpet. Which reminds me, I've got to pick him up in half an hour. Listen, give me a call when you get to town tomorrow. I want to get the Computease Amalgamated sewed up."

"What about Valentino's face-lift?"

"One thing at a time," Blake laughed.

"Roger and out."

After he hung up the phone, Blake arose quickly with his briefcase in hand, reached for his coat and headed for the outer office. "See you tomorrow, McGee," he said to his secretary.

She batted her eyes and smiled. Blake sighed. Even the fifty-five-year-old Edith McGee didn't seem immune to her boss's charm.

But he wasn't worried about McGee, Willy *or* Computease Amalgamated, which he'd just bought for a cool million. His thoughts centered on Alison Sherwood as he wondered if that dark-haired beauty would be like the other women in his life. With a jolt Blake reminded himself he was hiring her as a designer.

Blake wasn't the only parent late. Several kids who'd grown tired of waiting had started a snowball fight outside the music professor's Georgetown town house. A well-aimed, hard-packed snowball found its mark between

Blake's shoulder blades. The last thing he expected to see
on whirling around was a wide-eyed little girl who couldn't
have been more than six years old.

"I didn't do it!" she wailed and, thrusting an accusing
mitt at an older boy, said, "He did." With that, she
scooped up a handful of snow in defense.

"It was an accident, mister," the boy pleaded. "I was
aiming for him . . . and . . ."

"I got in the way," Blake supplied, a smile tugging at the
corners of his mouth. At least they'd taken his mind off
Ms. Sherwood.

"Hi, Dad." A tall redheaded boy stepped forward,
trumpet case in hand. "Did that twerp get you?" Thrusting the case into his father's hands, he pulled a snowball
from his jacket pocket and hurled it at the unsuspecting
boy.

"No fair!" the other boy shouted back, quickly pack-
ing one of his own, to a chorus of "Get him, get him!"
Most surprising was the blond-haired little girl who let out
a bloodcurdling shriek along with one of her snowballs.

Within minutes, sides had been redrawn, war hoops
sounded and the air was filled with icy missiles. "Better get
out of the way, Dad," Willy called. "It's the Sherwood
Gang!"

"I don't care if it's the Jets. C'mon, son, we need to get
home."

"One sec, Dad!" the boy shouted as he sent a volley of
balls into the enemy territory. Then, waving his hand, he
yelled, "Truce, truce! Time out!"

"Aw, Willy, jes' when it was getting good," the tall boy
with dark hair protested. A general rumble of displeasure
was heard as the others gathered around him. The rosy-
cheeked little girl defiantly stepped forward. "Best snow
all year and you have to be a sissy pants."

"Robin!" One of the brothers yanked her back and scolded her in low tones. "You want your mouth washed out with soap?"

"Pooh!" She tossed her blond braids. "We've never gotten our mouths washed out—you're just talk."

"There will be other snows," Blake assured them. He handed the trumpet case back to Willy and said, "Hop in. We're leaving Sherwood Forest."

"Aw, shucks." Willy made a face but reluctantly followed his father, then turning abruptly, called out, "See you guys later."

"I'm a *girl*, and my name's Robin!" The blond-haired child looked fiercely at Willy, who quickly ducked into the black Jaguar.

"She takes trumpet lessons, too?" Blake asked with mild curiosity as he started the car.

"Naw, she's too little. She just tags along sometimes." Rubbing frost from the windowpane, he added, "That must be their mom now." He whistled under his breath. "Wow, get a load of her!"

"Got to keep my eyes on the traffic, Willy." He shifted his gaze momentarily, in time to see the Sherwood Gang's mother slip behind the wheel of a packed station wagon. Blake heard himself suck in his breath, slam on the brakes and swear, all at the same time.

"Take it easy, Dad."

The station wagon pulled in front of him, and for a moment the woman stared directly into Blake's eyes. She looked as if she'd seen a ghost, then she snapped her head forward and stepped on the gas. In the back seat a dog that could have passed for a brontosaurus was licking the face of the little girl.

Blake could suddenly use a drink.

"Get ahold of yourself," Alison said out loud as she sped through an intersection.

"Hey, Mom, don't you obey traffic signs?" her eldest asked.

"I'm thirsty," Robin complained, giving the dog a shove and sinking into her seat.

"'Cause you ate all that snow, silly."

"Is not."

"Is so, and you'll probably get some disease like they talk about on TV."

"Will not!" Robin wailed.

"That'll be enough from you guys." Alison took a deep breath. It had been a long day, and seeing Valentino's double didn't help. Out of curiosity she idly asked, "Who was that tall kid you all were playing with?"

"Willy McLaughlin," they chorused, and Robin added, "He takes trumpet lessons, and he's older 'n better than Pete." She let out a squeal as her older brother punched her in the arm. "Make him stop!"

"Cut it out, Pete!" Alison sent a menacing look into the rearview mirror.

A preternatural calm settled over the back seat as the three children fell mute. Even the dog, after a single questioning bark, quieted, dropping his nose to his paws.

Silence. Blessed silence...more or less. The usual bleating of horns in the snow-snarled traffic, but at least they were moving up Wisconsin Avenue.

"McLaughlin..." Alison tested the name softly. It had a respectable ring to it. Surely he couldn't be the man from New Orleans, could he? Her cheeks burned with humiliation at the possibility.

She thought about him through supper, the dishes, and the *Post*'s crossword puzzle. Normally she could zip through it in an hour; tonight definitions teased the tip of her pencil. "A-c-r-o-n-y-m? Too many letters."

Looking up from the puzzle, her gaze swept the familiar living room. Antiques mingled cozily with Scandinavian modern, and Oriental rugs overlay shiny parquet floors. Cream-colored draperies covered the windows and, when drawn back, revealed a tiny but overgrown garden. Alison was strictly an *interior* designer. A grandfather clock ticked solemnly in the corner by the door, and dying embers popped and crackled on the wide hearth before them. The smell of wood smoke was pungent in the air.

It was a lovely house. She and Harry had bought it the same year he was killed in a freak car accident. Robin had still been a toddler, and so Alison's mother had moved in to help out. Had everything all happened only five years ago? It seemed much longer.

"A-c-r-o-n..." With a sigh of exasperation she tossed the paper down and announced, "I'm for bed."

"So early?" Her mother put aside the book she was reading and, peering over her bifocals, murmured, "That's not like you. Are you feeling well?"

"Just have a lot on my mind," Alison replied on a fake yawn. There was no way she'd let her mother know what had happened at Valentino's Pleasure. She had already given a detailed account of the designers' convention and had assured her that Sarah was doing well. Alison had finally found Sarah at an Italian restaurant, Valentino's, and after extracting a promise from her sister to keep in touch, returned to Washington, D.C. Although the embarrassment of her encounter at Valentino's Pleasure was never mentioned, her mother suspected something. At the slightest provocation, Marge O'Shaunnessey's little black bag of occult fix-its would be whipped out. It was never far from any crisis, be it Robin's scraped knee or Alison's love life. No gentleman caller escaped scrutiny. In the time it took to powder her nose, Marge could read a palm, check an aura and get vital statistics for an astrology chart.

"And I really think you ought to take a vacation."

Alison had caught the tail end of this advice, which had the ring of a doctor's prognosis. "But, Mom, I've just returned from New Orleans."

"I can imagine what kind of rest that must have been— a business convention and a short visit with Sarah." Marge reached out and clasped her daughter's hand. "I was thinking of something more in the line of a cruise. One of those package deals where you just trot down to the airlines and everything is handled. Think of it!" Her heavily made-up eyes rolled dramatically. "San Martin... Haiti...Greece..."

"Wrong continent," Alison laughed, giving an affectionate squeeze to her mother's hand. "Besides, I've got too much work to do—not to mention the possibility of the designer's showcase. That would really be a feather in my cap if I were among the chosen."

"Well, of course. And I've no doubt you'll be selected, but," her mother continued breathlessly, "that's not until next fall. In the meantime..."

"Maybe this summer..." Alison's voice trailed off as visions of white sandy beaches beckoned.

"Oh, but this summer will be too late!" Marge, looking like a cross between the queen mother and the Good Witch of the North shot to her feet. Tonight's outfit was a filmy lavender dress with a wispy boa, her trademark, at the neck. Matching lavender heels had been cast aside after dinner in favor of frothy mules. As always, jewelry jangled whenever she moved.

Alison let out a sigh as she saw the thick file clutched in her mother's hands. More about her astrological progressions, no doubt. It wouldn't be so galling if Marge made a few mistakes.

"Now," the older woman began as she settled next to her daughter on the Victorian love seat. "If my calculations are correct..." She flipped through reams of indecipherable pages. "Ah, yes. Your first night in New Orleans, something unusual happened." Blue eyes flashed and pinned a knowing look on Alison. "I'm getting quite proficient at my trances. I can find out without you telling me." She grinned wickedly.

"That's psychic blackmail!" Alison returned good-naturedly. "It'll build up nasty karma for you."

Marge's lips settled into a flat grim line. "You know just enough to be annoying. Oh, very well. I won't invade your privacy, but you really should confide in me. What are mothers for?" She shrugged one lavender-clad shoulder. "Despite what you think, I *am* trying to help you."

"Oh, I know you are, Mom, and I do appreciate it. But really, there's nothing to tell, and I'm beat. Got a new and picky client today, and Ingrid says we've got some really hot stuff coming up. Not only that, but since I'm running for president of the PTA they want me to go to the school board meeting tomorrow night."

Marge fluttered her eyelashes dramatically. "Like I said, you do too much! You should slow down so you can catch the beneficent rays the planets are showering on you! Jupiter and Venus are madly tossing goodies your way. I'm referring to your love life, and all you can think about is work and the PTA!"

"I know what you're hinting at, and as I've told you a hundred times, I'm not interested in forming a relationship right now."

"Pooh! I suppose you'll be perverse and wait for the Saturn square, or worse yet, the Neptune opposition and attract God-knows-what!"

Alison gave a snort of laughter. "If it makes you feel any better, I promise to be on the lookout for any heavenly prize, okay?"

"Well, that's somewhat reassuring. It's simply that you need a man in your life. Some romance, gaiety."

"Yes, Mama." Bending over, she gave Marge a kiss. "See you in the morning."

"Oh, I forgot to tell you, Hannah can't clean this week. She's enrolled in...um...that seminar. You know, the one I told you about—the past-life regressions." She tried out a smile on her daughter and quickly added, "She's certain that if she can just figure out who she was last time, then she can move to a higher income bracket and hire her own domestic!"

"Super!" Alison said with a hint of sarcasm.

"Now, don't worry. I've another girl coming. She'll be here Friday. Excellent references. In fact, I have it on good authority she practically cleans parquet floors with a toothbrush."

"Just so long as it isn't mine. Night, Mom, and thanks."

As Alison climbed the stairs, she heard Marge call out, "And she's a triple Pisces. Just imagine!"

Sleep seemed to take forever to come. Though it was Alison's second night home, she couldn't forget the man from Valentino's. She had insulted him and made a fool of herself in the process. When would she learn to get ahold of her temper?

Turning on her side, Alison punched her pillow down, sighed and waited for exhaustion to overtake her. Perhaps she did need a real vacation. She'd only had one since

Harry had died, and that had been to the Bahamas. A storm had come up and the deluxe cruise was spent below deck. So much for cruises.

Alison let out another sigh as fluorescent pink flamingos flashed against the inky blackness of her closed lids. If Sarah had just let someone know where she was moving. If she'd only bothered to mention that Valentino's was an Italian restaurant. Sometimes life seemed to hinge on probables.

Head-in-the-clouds Sarah, so like their mother. Thankfully Alison had taken after their father, an architect, who had died of a heart attack just before Sarah was born. Alison was ten at the time and had adored him.

Wiping away unexpected tears, she turned once more in bed. The two men she had loved the most had died so abruptly and so young. There were times when Alison wondered if she was afraid to love again. After all, there hadn't been anyone since Harry had died. Yet it was this very tragedy that brought out her own strengths, that drove her to become one of the top designers in Washington, D.C. Alison had convinced herself that there just hadn't been time for love.

As she drifted off to sleep, images of a dark-eyed man floated before her.

"It's a good thing you made reservations," Alison said as the maître d' swept them past the agitated lunchtime crowd.

"Window seats, *mademoiselles*." Snapping the menu open, he assured them a waiter would be along momentarily.

"I know what I want," Alison said, glancing at the special. "*Crêpes à la Crème*, a glass of dry red wine and..." craning her neck in the direction of the pastry cart, she continued, "something fattening."

"Might as well make that two," her assistant, Ingrid Johnson, said, laying the menu to one side. "Believe it or not, Ted gave me a five-pound box of Godiva chocolates for Valentine's Day, so I have no cause to mourn love's labor lost." Ingrid leaned forward. "A few pounds should be more like it, but *c'est la vie*. Ted likes the Rubenesque look." With a toss of her honey-blond curls, she added, "So, what's your excuse for this splurge? Not that you have to worry."

Between the wine and the crepes, Alison summarized the fiasco in New Orleans.

"You mean you just walked out of Valentino's?"

"More or less," Alison replied as the crepes arrived.

"You should have stuck around. Sounded like the beginning of an interesting evening. You didn't even get his name?"

"Afraid not."

Ingrid blinked. "You're out of practice."

"Now don't start in. If you'd been in that sleaze joint, you might have reacted the same." Alison took a bite of the crepe before continuing. "I mean, neon-lit pink flamingos as window dressing?" She gave a wicked smile. "With sequined G-strings in their mouths."

"You mean beaks?" Ingrid teased.

"Beaks...mouths...whatever."

"Let's talk about this mystery man some more."

"Let's not."

"But he sounds intriguing. Rich, handsome..." Ingrid plunged her fork into the crepes, withdrew a succulent mushroom and, brandishing it at Alison, said, "Because what you need is a man."

"You sound like Mom."

"Well, a word to the wise is sufficient." Ingrid waved the fork like a wand and added, "As usual, you look fabulous."

"Thanks." Unconsciously Alison plucked at the black angora sweater. A single strand of pearls and matching earrings were the only accessories. Her thick dark hair, fashioned into a Gibson girl, softly framed her oval face. After a moment Alison defended herself with, "But I *do* date. It's not as if I hide in a shell."

"I don't know about that," Ingrid countered. "Then I suppose if you consider PTA meetings as the hot social item of the month..."

"You really *are* as bad as Mom!" Alison laughed.

"I'm surprised she hasn't found your soul mate for you," Ingrid teased as she scraped the last vestiges of food from her plate.

"Don't suggest it."

"Marge's okay with me. Any man who passes her litmus test is definitely playing with a full deck. Hey, I'm in the mood for a napoleon, how 'bout you?"

"I think I can make room," Alison said with a laugh as she plucked two pastries from the cart. "Now let's shelve my love life and talk about this new client."

"I've been saving him for dessert." Ingrid's eyes twinkled mischievously.

"That bad."

"I looked his bio up today." She whistled softly.

"Go on," Alison prompted impatiently.

"He's a self-made millionaire from Texas with a company worth millions and holdings in nearly every major industry. He's about forty-four years old, works out at a spa three times a week, looks like a young Gregory Peck and is considered to be one of the least known eligible bachelors in America."

"I see your wheels turning, Ingrid Johnson. First the man in Valentino's—"

"Hold on to your hat. This dream boat lives in your backyard."

Alison held a forkful of napoleon midair. "Year-round?"

"Oh, well, he has other places. You know how the superrich are. When they get bored, they change houses."

"Must be nice," Alison sighed. "It's all I can do to keep mine running. Sometimes I feel like a zookeeper. Just last week all of Eric's snakes escaped, and we've only found five."

Ingrid waved her hand in front of Alison's face. "Have you been listening to me?"

"Every word. But it's too good to be true; you know how PR is. Besides, I don't really want to change houses when I get bored."

"You're sublimating," Ingrid warned.

"The word you want is *suppressing*, and you're right, I am. So, when am I supposed to drop in on this Adonis?"

"His secretary said he's booked tomorrow, so I set it up tentatively for the day after at eleven in the morning."

"Eleven? That's right before lunch."

"What better way to inaugurate a business arrangement than over a nice leisurely repast?"

"Ingrid Johnson, you're too much. Playing Cupid at your age. The man's probably married with a dozen children." Sighing, she pushed the dessert plate from her. "That was delicious."

"You *weren't* listening. I said 'bachelor,' though I think I read he was widowed. I do know he's unattached."

"His name?"

"Blake McLaughlin."

Alison grew thoughtful for a moment, then ventured softly, "This McLaughlin wouldn't happen to have a teenage son who plays the trumpet, would he?"

"Do I look like Sherlock Holmes?" Motioning for the check, Ingrid said, "My treat."

Chapter Two

Maybe her mother was right, Alison thought as she raced up the steps to the school board meeting; perhaps she was doing too much. But being elected president of the PTA meant so much to her. It wasn't a crazy idea, despite what Marge said, especially since Alison's three children were at Mallory Elementary. There were issues that needed to be dealt with—everything from drugs to improved school lunches—and Alison felt she was the best candidate to head the PTA and implement these changes.

She took a deep breath as she reached the top of the thirty-five steps leading to the entrance of Mallory Elementary. Great exercise, especially when you're lugging a bulging briefcase. She pushed through the glass-and-metal doors, took one look at the hall clock, let out a sigh and hurried down the corridor. She'd never been to a school board meeting and was ten minutes late. At least she looked her part—respectable and yet chic—though the time it took to change from her black sweater dress to the burgundy wool suit had eaten up ten minutes. Of course that wouldn't have been necessary if Payowakit, their black Persian cat, hadn't thrown up in her lap.

Naturally the meeting had begun. As she opened the squeaky door, there was a moment of silence and all heads swung around to stare at her. Sally Freemantle, the current PTA president smiled warmly and patted a chair beside her.

"We've just begun," the matronly woman whispered. "Mr. Thacker is going over the budget." She lowered her voice even further to add, "It's a small board and none of them are long-winded, so it'll be an early evening."

Alison quietly slipped out of her cape and gave a cursory glance at the board members who sat at the round table. They were pleasant looking and all in their thirties and forties. Four women and four men. At least they believed in ERA. Alison's speculations came to an abrupt halt as she locked eyes with the man opposite her. How could she have missed him? She blinked as if the vision might change. He merely stared back with those jet-black eyes she remembered all too well. A single eyebrow was raised in her direction.

What was "Valentino" doing on the school board? Alison swallowed the lump in her throat but found herself unable to look away. The man in the black Jaguar? Willy McLaughlin's father? The Texas millionaire? Impossible. There must be some mistake. He simply couldn't be the man from New Orleans! Things like that only happened in books and movies.

Pulling her gaze away, Alison withdrew a legal pad from her briefcase and nervously made a pretense of writing something on the yellow foolscap. Anything! "February 25th" was good for starters. She sneaked a look at him. A curious smile was etched on his face. She thought of their meeting in Valentino's, of the red swing and all those filmy negligees, of the music and the pulsating lights. To her chagrin she was blushing. She glanced back at the pad before her. "School Board Meeting," she hastily wrote, underlining it for emphasis, but her thoughts were a thousand miles away, remembering her hurled insults at a total stranger and her rapid retreat from the den of iniquity.

The meeting was proceeding with predictability, but the jarring presence of Blake McLaughlin kept her on the edge of her chair. When he was finally introduced to her, she felt her insides do a slow flip-flop.

He, on the other hand, was smoothness and light, and as chairman of Ways and Means, gave an update capsule much as a late-night newscaster—one with definitely high ratings.

"You know who *he* is," Sally whispered as he sat down amid rustling of papers.

"Blake McLaughlin," Alison managed to reply without stammering. "Millionaire entrepreneur," she added with a shrug. Let Sally Freemantle go into ecstasy. She was a sweet but sadly ineffectual PTA president, who was quite eager to give up her chair.

"Ah, then you know!" Sally winked, then quickly composed herself as the board chairman asked for her report from Mallory Elementary. As usual she glossed over the important issues and concentrated on the upcoming spring bazaar and the bake contest. Having won hands down last year for her double-fudge pecan cake, she had a vested interest in the event. Her other achievement during the past year was the inclusion of monthly school lunches at Fast Freddy's Fried Chicken. An occasional napoleon was one thing, but a steady diet of junk food for growing children was another. In this respect Alison and her mother shared similar views.

'And now, I'd like to introduce our nominee for next year's president of our PTA, Alison Sherwood, who, as a mother of three, has a specific topic of importance to address, one which is of concern to us all.''

There was a scattering of applause, and Alison was on her feet, smiling mechanically and wondering how she was going to get through her brief remarks. Clutching her index cards gave her hands something to do to keep them from trembling. She simply wouldn't look at Blake McLaughlin; she'd pretend he wasn't there. That was trickier than she thought. The man kept his unnerving gaze pinned on her, the barest hint of a smile on his lips. Thankfully, Alison's talk introducing her intentions for next year was only two minutes long. However, when she touched on the issue of cracking down on pornography, with the help of congressional legislation, she noticed Mr. McLaughlin sit forward with a look of interest on his face. Alison, feeling her own face color slightly, brought her talk to a speedy close.

"You brought up some excellent points, Mrs. Sherwood." Blake McLaughlin tapped his pencil on the table for emphasis, and, slanting a dark look at Alison, added, "You've got my vote."

This accolade was repeated by other members, and after calling for order, the board president asked if there was further business. There wasn't, so the meeting dissolved into a hum of chatter. Alison, determined to avoid Blake, was moving rapidly toward the door when Sally Freemantle hooked elbows with her and neatly steered her back into the hub of activity.

"I brought some Danishes from the deli. You'll simply have to have one!" She plopped one on a paper plate and thrust it into Alison's hands.

"Thanks, but I've had my pastry for the day," she protested lightly, all too aware of Blake's presence.

"Nonsense. You're too thin," the older woman countered. She flashed a smile at Blake and added, "She's one of those vegetarians, poor thing. What she really needs is a good steak, potatoes and gravy."

"I think Mrs. Sherwood looks fine," he murmured, his dark eyes raking over Alison's figure. At that, Sally Freemantle sputtered something, grabbed her own Danish and, nibbling one gooey edge, retreated for coffee.

"I might also add, you get around." His smile was genuine. Taking the unwanted Danish off Alison's plate, he said, "I'll bet you drink decaf, right?"

"Swiss water-processed, when available," she replied with a nervous laugh. Then gesturing to the coffee urn, she said, "Sanka does fine in a pinch."

"Allow me," he said deftly. "One lump or two?" A twinkle lit up his eye, "Though I expect you avoid sugar, too."

"Not all the time, but I do take my coffee black." She accepted the cup graciously, blowing on the steaming contents and wondering what would happen next.

"As you can see, I really am most respectable," Blake offered after a moment.

"So am I," Alison laughed, feeling more at ease yet still a bit unnerved at finding Valentino on the school board.

"There was never a moment's doubt in my mind. When last we met, you were quite clear about that." He paused to sip his coffee and study her. The fact that they were surrounded by people didn't seem to faze him.

"I apologize for my...erratic behavior. I'm not usually so vocal with total strangers. I hope you understand."

"Not completely. I am a little curious as to why you were in Valentino's in the first place." He added cream to his coffee and looked at her, one eyebrow raised, in the expectant manner of one used to getting explanations.

"Would you believe I was there looking for my younger sister? I feared she was working there, but she turned out to be at Valentino's Pizzeria. After making a fool of myself, I didn't feel like sticking around to explain."

"I'd have been delighted if you had." The smile he gave her above the rim of his coffee cup vanished as if he'd suddenly tasted poison. "I am being presumptuous." He flexed his wrist and looked at his handsome gold watch. "It's also getting rather late, and I expect you have your hands full. That was you I saw with the station wagon load of kids last night, wasn't it?"

"Yes, and you're right, I'd better get home." She finished the last of the Sanka, dropped the paper cup into the trash and slipped into her red cape. Blake McLaughlin was everything Ingrid had said, and more. But if Alison's sixth sense was on target, she realized she'd better steer clear of him while she still could. He had the kind of looks that would grow on her: cool, guarded, with a white-hot fire beneath that would burn and leave scars. Thank you, she would go home, have a nice cup of chamomile tea and a rice cracker, watch the eleven-o'clock news and go off to dreamland. As far as the design contract with him, like Scarlett O'Hara, she'd think about that tomorrow.

"Good night," she called out to the remaining board members. Sally, whose mouth was full of Danish, looked disappointedly from Alison to Blake. Alison sighed. Marge, Ingrid and now Sally, matchmakers all!

As usual the morning was heralded with the chaos of shrieking children and howling animals. Alison escaped to jog half of her regular distance because it had started to sleet with a vengeance, and, on top of yesterday's now-sooty snow, roads were less than appealing.

What to do about Mr. McLaughlin? she pondered as her station wagon plowed through rush-hour traffic. On nice days she usually walked the six blocks to her Georgetown office, but weather notwithstanding, she had to pick up some supplies that afternoon.

Her design studio, located on the main thoroughfare of Wisconsin Avenue was sandwiched between a high-priced boutique and a jewelry store specializing in contemporary pieces. The door to Alison's studio sported a brass name-plate that simply read Georgetown Interiors. She had played the Georgetown theme to the hilt, decorating the reception area in antique love seats and Oriental carpets. Down a narrow hall were the brightly lit and streamlined studios.

"Ingrid," Alison called out as she entered the first studio, "how would you like to take on the McLaughlin account?"

Her assistant looked up from the drawing board. "Are you kidding? I've got to finish Mrs. Chumley's solarium. Besides, this is your plum, remember?" She tossed Alison a knowing look before returning to her rendering.

"I couldn't be more serious," Alison assured her as she hung up her cape. "The fact is, I met Mr. McLaughlin last night."

"Yeah?" Ingrid's head snapped up. "How did you accomplish that?"

"He's on the school board, that's how. You might as well know, my mind's made up. I don't want to do the job. It's all yours. After all, we're partners, aren't we?"

"Flattery won't work. I'm your assistant, who's just starting out in the field, and I'm here to learn from you,

O wise one. So, tell me, what has Prince Charming done to cause this reaction in you?''

"To begin with, he's not the casual bachelor you said—"

"Widowed. Go on." Ingrid swiveled on her chair and stared expectantly at Alison.

"Aside from his marital status, he happens to be one and the same as the man in New Orleans!" With a sigh she eased herself onto a stool and looked vacantly into space before adding, "So, you see I just can't do this job."

"You're telling me Blake McLaughlin is the new owner of that . . . sex shop?"

"Exactly. He's selling it, so at least he's got some scruples. But I don't want to work for him! He makes me feel uncomfortable."

"That's a new word for it! Okay, okay, never mind. But tell me this, what possible harm can it do for you to redecorate this man's office? Move a couple of potted plants around, change the color of his walls. You can do it blindfolded!"

"So can you. It'll be a good experience for you."

"Ditto for you! I'd imagine you'd jump at the chance to redesign a corporate president's office. Remember the woman from Georgia who redid some bigwig's Rosslyn office? Got reviewed in the 'Style' section of the *Post*. Now that kind of publicity can't hurt us, can it?"

"You do the McLaughlin job and get the write-up in the *Post*!" Alison slid off the stool and headed for her studio, Ingrid fast on her heels.

"Okay, if I agree to do the design work, you make the initial contact." This remark stopped Alison in her tracks.

"I don't want to make any more contact, period. I'd just as soon he didn't know this is my company."

"You mean he doesn't know who you are?"

"Well, he knows I'm Alison Sherwood and that I have three children and am running for president of the PTA. That's enough."

"You're afraid the poor man can't take the shock of learning your profession?" Ingrid shook her head in amazement. "All because of a mix-up in some sex shop in New Orleans? Come on, Alison, who're you kidding? You've run away from every eligible man who's come on the horizon. It's time to crack that shell you've encased yourself in!"

"I don't know what you're talking about," Alison hedged defensively.

"Let me get something straight. McLaughlin didn't insult you, make a lewd pass or commit any other socially unacceptable act, right?" At Alison's reluctant nod, she continued, "Yet you've taken a vow to steer clear of the man as if he were a monster. You know what I think? You're running from something inside you."

"Oh, Ingrid, don't be silly. You and Mom must be taking the same self-help seminars." Flipping open her appointment book, she made a pretense of searching for a phone number. She didn't need to be psychoanalyzed, especially not at nine in the morning. Like Marge, Ingrid had an uncanny way of zeroing in on a problem, which was fine in business, but not in Alison's personal life. Looking up, she said, "I do appreciate your concern, but believe me, I'm not running from anything, except possible trouble."

"Sometimes trouble can teach us a lot."

"I've taken the graduate course." Alison laughed, then added quickly, "But since you set up the appointment, you meet with him!"

"Then you *do* agree to do the job."

Alison hesitated before she shrugged and said, "I suppose I can handle it."

"You bet you can!" Ingrid sang out on her exit.

Of course Alison could handle it, she reassured herself. After all, she was a thirty-eight-year-old adult. A widow with three children. Then she groaned. The simple fact was she hadn't met a man as compelling as Blake since Harry died. Yes, it frightened her. But no, she wasn't running. There just wasn't room in her life for the inevitable heartbreak that love seemed to bring. After Harry had died, she thought the loneliness would last forever. Of course, it didn't, but if she hadn't had three small children looking to her for love and support, she probably would have gone over the edge. So what if she'd built a protective wall around herself. It had gotten her on her feet and made her the success she was today. And no man, not even Blake McLaughlin, could take that away from her.

Looking down at her hands, she noticed they were gripping the appointment book with such an intensity that her knuckles were white. She released her hold and reassured herself she was not running from love. After all, she had a full life with her family and work. Wasn't that enough?

Obsession was the clinical term, but no matter how Blake labeled his feelings, the fact was he couldn't get Ms. Sherwood off his mind. *Mrs.* Sherwood, he reminded himself as he glanced at her business card once again. He probably should have told her last night that he'd hired her as his designer, but he hadn't. She was married, had three kids and was damn attractive. These thoughts were interrupted by a buzz from the intercom and McGee's announcement that a Ms. Johnson from Georgetown Interiors had arrived.

"Johnson, you say?" He paused momentarily before abruptly adding, "Send her in." Leaning back in his leather chair, he scrutinized the door, his eyes narrowing slightly, his fingers steepled before him.

The woman who appeared was definitely not Alison! Though she had that same straightforward look in her eye, the similarities stopped there. Ms. Johnson was a plump blonde who, if Blake's guess was on target, stood at an even five feet.

"Ingrid Johnson," she said, stepping forward, one hand extended, the other gripping a portfolio.

Blake rose, shook her hand and said after a moment, "I appreciate your coming over, but I was under the impression I was dealing with Ms. Sherwood." His lips curved in one of his dangerous smiles. Obviously Alison put two and two together and decided to back off. He'd see about that!

"Oh, yes. You will be, but I'm just here to go through the initial paperwork." She paused, blinked expectantly at Blake and hurried on. "I've brought samples of Ms. Sherwood's work, and—"

"I'm aware of her work, which is why I engaged her." He rounded the edge of his desk, annoyed that the woman hadn't kept her appointment. "You see," he added in a softer tone, "there are some things I specifically want done. So, since Ms. Sherwood is too busy to come here, I'll just go to her."

"Oh, but she's...she's...." Ingrid slapped the portfolio on Blake's desk as an offering. "She's very—"

"Busy, I'm sure. But I won't take too much of her time." He felt some of his humor return. Crossing toward the door, he said over his shoulder, "Perhaps you'd like to come and take notes?"

"Although I'd love to, I think you and Ms. Sherwood had best meet alone." There was a definite sparkle in the blonde's eye, one that piqued Blake's curiosity.

Any misgivings Blake had entertained as he crossed the crowded Key Bridge were swept aside after a maddening search for a parking place, which he finally found on one of Georgetown's icy side streets. Undoubtedly, Ms. Johnson was having a similar problem, for he'd lost sight of her car some time back. He knew where Georgetown Interiors was located, but wasn't prepared for the narrow and very steep staircase that led to Alison's office. He took the steps two at a time, feeling an unaccustomed rush of adrenaline pump through his veins. She's married, he reminded himself for the tenth time that day as he paused before entering her office.

Soft classical music filled the air, and a vase of flowers on the marble mantelpiece scented the office with the promise of spring. His gaze took in a cozy enclave of high-backed antique love seats upholstered in a soft peach velvet. The floor was covered with beautifully patterned Oriental rugs, and a low-lying glass coffee table held several issues of *Architectural Digest*. He called out Alison's name and was answered by a faint echo from the high-ceilinged room.

Alerted by a sound behind him, he whirled around in time to collide with her.

"Blake!" she cried out, nearly dropping her carryout Chinese lunch. "Oh, you practically sacred me to death!" Regaining her composure, she added, "What are you doing *here*? Ingrid's supposed to be—"

"Giving me the kiss-off?" he said with a laugh. "Not quite. And by the way, do you always leave your office unlocked and unattended?" In the momentary silence that fell, Blake let his gaze quickly travel over her. Instead of her usual topknot, her thick dark hair was swept into a classic French roll. The simplicity brought into focus her deep green eyes that stared back at him in surprise. Her navy-and-white houndstooth suit was both chic and businesslike. A shimmering red silk blouse added the perfect touch of femininity. Blake heard his own intake of breath. He didn't usually notice such details in a woman. "Well?" he added after a moment, "Because if I'd been a robber—"

"Were that the case," Alison said, reclaiming her composure, "you'd have wonton soup and egg roll all over that nice charcoal coat!" She grinned wickedly, for despite everything, the man had more charm than the law should allow. Even though he made her feel uncomfortable, she *was* drawn to him!

"I suppose you *can* defend yourself," he conceded on a laugh. "Still, you gave up an appointment with me to have Chinese carryout?"

Alison neatly skirted the question and, starting down the hall, fired one back at him, "You knew who I was last night, didn't you?"

"I would have said something," he lied, following her into her studio, "but you disappeared."

"*I* disappeared?"

"Indeed." His mouth twitched. "All the way from Cotton Candi—it *was* Cotton Candi, wasn't it?—to president of the PTA. Quite versatile, *and* my designer. Fate is wonderful, isn't it?"

"Fate?" Alison choked on the word. Pulling out her lunch, she apologized, "I'm afraid there won't be quite enough to go around." She settled into her chair before saying, "I've given it some consideration and think that perhaps you would work better with Ms. Johnson, although since you're here we can set up the contract."

"Then this is your business?" he asked unexpectedly.

"Well, yes. I started Georgetown Interiors five years ago when... I needed a little self-expression," she said on a purposefully light note. "But getting back to the coincidence of your choosing me as your designer—"

"I confess!" He paused as a devilish gleam lit up his eyes. He pushed her business card across her desk and said, "You dropped this in Valentino's Pleasure." His voice grew more serious. "But the fact remains, I *do* need a good designer."

"I'm flattered, but—"

"You're too busy?" His eyes settled on the Chinese lunch.

"As a matter of fact," Alison continued, groping for a reasonable explanation, "this job is perfect for Ms. Johnson, who's been looking for just such a challenge."

"Ah, then you're both familiar with the job and you're right, it is a challenge." Magnanimously he added, "Please, don't let me keep you from your chop suey."

"Wonton soup and egg roll," she corrected. Alison suppressed a grin as she removed the lid from the steaming cup of soup. "I still feel that Ms. Johnson would—"

"My company wishes specifically to work with you."

"That's impossible," Alison said, thankful that Ingrid wasn't there to complicate things. "You see, I've made all the arrangements with my assistant to handle the job."

"Nothing's impossible! Camelot Enterprises wants the head designer, not an assistant." He was smiling again. "It will be well worth your while. Perhaps the fee could be augmented."

"It's really out of the question, Mr. McLaughlin. My schedule is too full." She tried to sound firm, not petulant. "I'm sure you understand," she tacked on.

"Completely," he agreed breezily. "Children, PTA and dogs have a prior claim. It happens to a lot of women."

"That's not the problem at all!" she heard herself snap. Hands clenched and sucking in her breath, she added in measured tones, "You obviously have a patronizing opinion of women."

"Not at all. It's not easy being wife, mother and holding down a career. Superwoman is the term, I believe."

Alison felt spots of color bloom on her cheeks. It was ridiculous! She'd blushed more since meeting Blake McLaughlin then she'd done in her entire life. The man had a decidedly unsettling effect on her. He'd even managed to chase away her hunger. With a sigh she pushed the soup to one side. "I am not competing for supermom. The fact is my schedule is—"

"I know, booked. Well, unbook it a little. For I'd thought Ms. Johnson had said you'd be the designer."

"Well, I changed my mind."

Flipping to her calender in defense, Alison was about to add something when Blake said very softly, "Pencil me in."

"You don't take no for an answer, do you?"

"One of my failings." He offered her a twisted smile. "I don't imagine your husband likes your schedule. I know I wouldn't." His smile broadened momentarily, then snapped back to a tight line.

It was on the tip of Alison's tongue to correct his misconception of her marital status, but recognizing the banked fires in his dark eyes, she decided to let it pass. She looked pensively at the gold band on her third finger and realized with a jolt she wore it like armor.

Rising, Blake crossed to her drawing board and asked, "Mind if I look?"

She nodded, once again feeling a little bested by the man.

"Very nice," he murmured after a moment. "You're a woman of many talents, and I definitely want you to do the design work." He paused to study a particular rendering. "I like your flair."

"Thank you, but I stand firm."

"So do I. It will be you or no one." His eyes were on her again, mesmerizing pools of darkness that refused denial. "Besides, you've seen what you'll be working from. You *do* remember Valentino's, don't you?"

"Is that what this job is? I thought you were selling it! Mr. McLaughlin, if you think—"

"I think we've met often enough for you to call me Blake."

"Valentino's Pleasure is not the kind of place I wish to risk my professional reputation on."

"I'll double your fee."

"You really are stubborn, aren't you?"

"You call it stubborn, I call it determined," he replied smoothly.

"Harry used to say that—" She caught herself in mid-sentence.

"Harry?" he prompted. "Your husband?"

"Yes, my husband." Nervously she turned back to the designs. She was a terrible liar.

A look of realization settled on Blake's face. "I'd like to meet him sometime, that is, if he's around."

Alison took a steadying breath, "Well, he's not. I can see what you're thinking, that I led you to believe he was—"

"You still wear a ring."

"In memory," she said softly.

"I'm sorry." His voice was sincere, and after a moment he crossed the room and sat quietly opposite her.

"He died when my youngest was an infant."

Blake looked at her without saying a thing. His expression was as unreadable as stone. He was about to say something when his beeper went off. Pulling it from his breast pocket, he flicked a switch and spoke into it, "Yes, McGee?"

"Lew Mathieson's at The Iron Fence. Says it's important you meet him there for lunch."

"Tell him to give me twenty minutes." He clicked off, looked up at Alison and said, "Can't get out of this one. He's our attorney. Tell you what, don't decide on anything now. Think about it, then we can meet later and discuss the job. Say, dinner tonight? That is, if you can get away from the Sherwood Gang. I believe that was how my son referred to your children."

In spite of everything, Alison laughed. "Yes, that's how they bill themselves. Actually, my mother lives with us and loves to take care of them."

"Undoubtedly a courageous woman. How does seven-thirty sound? Give you enough time to feed all those hungry mouths?"

"Oh, yes." Nervously she twisted the band of gold on her left hand. His presence was making her feel light-headed.

"Good!" Blake rose and added, "Your little girl's quite outspoken."

"She takes after me," Alison heard herself reply.

"A real fighter." he started for the door, sporting a victory grin, then paused to say, "Oh, I'll need your address."

"Of course! It's easy to find." Withdrawing her card, she turned it over and quickly wrote the address. Handing it to him, she said, "Go up Wisconsin Avenue to R Street, turn right and take the next right. When you get to Tulip Lane, keep an ear out for screaming kids."

"Sounds like heaven," he remarked casually. "Tell me, do your children have any idea of your multifaceted career?"

"Full-time fans, Mr. McLaughlin," she parried, all too aware of the tremor in her voice.

"Blake will do fine." His gaze made her feel a little weak in the knees, like a marionette whose strings had just been clipped. Well, at least Ingrid would be happy.

Even though Blake lived in Georgetown, he hated its incessant traffic. Suddenly he could have cared less. He said her name to himself as he idled at a particularly long stoplight. Alison Sherwood aka Cotton Candi and PTA Mom of the Year. He shook his head. The light finally changed and he inched ahead, all too aware of the ridiculous grin on his face as he reflected on the irony of Alison's redesigning Valentino's. He felt an unexpected drum of excitement, remembering his first encounter with her. It was an odd contrast to the woman he'd just seen. Yet beneath that tailored suit was a soft silk blouse with pearl buttons. And beneath that . . . He could almost feel the crush of fabric in his hands, the buttons between his fingers. Get a grip on yourself! he silently commanded. The wail of a nearby siren jolted Blake McLaughlin from further speculation. The important thing was that the woman could do the job.

His thoughts ricocheted around his head through lunch. Lew, quick to spot ripples in a pond, commented on this over martinis. "It's a woman, isn't it?"

"You've been watching too many old movies," Blake countered, toying with a drunken olive on a swizzle stick.

"What's she like?"

"I'll let you know when I find out." He popped the olive into his mouth and swallowed it down with the martini.

"You pay me for advice, right?" Lew took a handful of salted nuts and slid the dish across the table.

"Correct, counselor. But only for corporate affairs."

"End of discussion, eh? Very well, Blake." Giving the menu a cursory glance, he added, "I'm having bluefish with baked potatoes and peas. How 'bout you? Gonna drink your lunch?"

Blake shot his longtime friend and lawyer a disbelieving look. "I've got more respect for my liver than that. I'll have the same." He snapped the menu closed with the air of shelving their previous discussion. "Now let's talk business."

"Right," Lew said. "It's a business lunch, let's stick to essentials. The order of the day is Computease Amalgamated, which as I said stands to make your company a bundle. I've also got the stuff on Valentino's, which is extensive."

"Fire away," Blake muttered, draining the martini glass.

"Children! Children! When this nice man comes to take your mother out, I want you on your best behavior. Is that understood?" Marge gave an ecstatic clap of her hands as she whirled in Alison's direction and announced regally, "The aspects are unusually turbulent this evening, *but* that can also forebode a certain excitement. *N'est-ce pas?*"

"I'm stimulated enough," Alison assured her mother as she fastened a gold earring in place. "And please, Mama, don't barrage the man with, well, you know."

"I shall be discreet, never fear."

All three children swung their gazes up from the TV and snickered. At the sound of the doorbell, Eric, the next to youngest, sprang up. "It's for me! 'Sides, it's too early for Dream Boat!"

"Eric Sherwood, you watch that tongue of yours!" Marge called out in vain as the ten-year-old swooped past her, grabbing a handful of cookies and a baseball bat. "And put your coat on, or you'll catch your death!"

"It's not cold!" he yelled back, then giving an ear-splitting whistle, called the dog. A black Persian cat, who'd been napping on top of the wing chair, hissed loudly and swung a defiant claw in Eric's direction. The dog, a mammoth mongrel, galumphed out the door with Eric.

"Now you've upset Payowakit!" Marge scolded as she stroked the bristling black cat.

Robin jumped up from the couch and marched into the kitchen. "She misses her kitties."

"No, leave them in the box!" Alison called out, a note of panic creeping into her voice. "We've got a man coming over to look at them."

Robin reappeared with three squirming balls of multi-colored fur, huge ears and slanted eyes. "They're so pretty," she said silkily, depositing them in the wing chair. "Come, Payowakit, your babies miss you!" Payowakit yawned with decided disinterest.

"If only she hadn't gotten out," Marge commented on a tragic note. "We could have had pedigree Persians instead of...these."

"They're cute," Robin cooed. Kneeling on the floor, she tried to coax the recalcitrant mother down.

"Adorable," Alison sighed, brushing lint from the skirt of a dark green knit. "But we can't keep them, and you know that."

"I don't see why not," Robin said plaintively.

"'Cause we got *too* many animals," Pete mimicked his mother's usual rejoinder as he grabbed his pitcher's mitt and started for the door. "Not to mention all of Eric's snakes that are slithering around. I'm gonna see where the action's at."

"Dinner in fifteen minutes," Marge announced. Drawing her daughter toward the couch, she said, "Tell me more about this new client of yours, McLaughlin, I believe you said his name is."

Her response was drowned out by a howl from the kitchen. "Oh, my God! It's Studs and Playboy!"

"Dear, dear," her mother uttered as Alison dashed from the room. "As soon as Cousin Tom is settled, he's bound to come for them. Sagittarians love animals. If only they weren't so hard to pin down."

Blake had no trouble finding the house, though the screaming kids were not immediately evident. Nevertheless, he sensed imminent mayhem lurked beyond the well-cleared walk. The house of modest Federal architecture was red brick with forest-green shutters. Amber light poured from small-paned windows, and gaslight flickered off its brick facade. Against the side of the house, he saw bicycles, a scooter and a lone tricycle, which would belong to the feisty Robin. The phrase, hell on wheels, seemed appropriate if not a little disconcerting. Like mother, like daughter. Wasn't that the way Alison put it?

A thud of something very hard hit him on the chest the moment he stepped from his Jaguar. Out of nowhere, four, five, six boys of all ages materialized, and, like specters out of a Grade B horror movie, they frosted up the air with panting breaths.

"Gee, mister. Are you all right?"

Ah, that familiar voice, Blake thought. One of the little Sherwoods. "What's this, the welcome wagon?" he asked in a constrained voice. Bending over, he retrieved the baseball.

"Hey, Pete, that's Willy's father," one of the children buzzed. "What's *he* doing here?"

"The last time," Blake began, tossing the ball into the air, "I got it in the back with a snowball. I returned to even it out. Didn't know this was baseball season, though."

"It ain't," one voice answered.

"Isn't," another corrected.

"Here's your ball." Blake threw it toward the tallest boy, the one with dark hair who seemed to be in charge. Alison Sherwood's eldest. "I'm just going to the front door, and I'm unarmed." No sooner had he said this than a furry dog came full throttle out of nowhere, threw himself on Blake and began licking him as if he were a bone.

"He won't hurt you, sir," Pete assured him, grappling for the animal's collar. "Besides, he's had his rabies shots. Down, Dog! Down. Good Dog. Now sit!" He flashed Blake a smile. "Dog went to obedience school, but he's still got a ways to go." Dog was straining at the collar, eager for more fun with the stranger.

"It might help if you gave him a name." Blake brushed at the distinct paw prints on his coat.

"He's got a name. Dog."

"Dog?"

"Dog. Mom named him. Marge wanted to call him 'Grand Master,' but Mom said, 'No way!'" This seemed to amuse the boy, who with Dog and an entourage of neighborhood urchins, followed Blake up the porch steps. This peculiar honor guard did not, however, steer him clear of an errant skate. He went flying into the front door, in one piece and still standing, but shaken, to say the least.

A chorus of "Gee, mister" surrounded him as the door was whipped open. Robin, who must have been lying in wait, made a dramatic moment of discovering him, her hand clapped to her mouth, eyes rolling and gasping appropriately.

"Gee, mister," she finally said, stepping back.

Was that all these Sherwoods knew how to say? Blake wondered. Children and dogs everywhere. Lord, there had to be more than one canine. Above the pandemonium, he heard Robin chatter, "Marge, Marge! The big cheese is here!" The girl was jumping up and down as if something were biting her. Fleas, perhaps.

"Robin Sherwood! Where are your manners?"

Blake looked up to see a swirl of pink with a matching boa and the most incredible red-hennaed hair he'd ever seen. It had to be Alison's mother.

"Those of you who don't belong here, home!" Bejeweled fingers flashed in the porch light. "The rest of you, wash for dinner." Settling her gaze on Blake, she murmured, "My heavens, what happened to you?"

"A baseball, a dog and a skate. No broken bones, though."

"I should hope not!" With a sweeping gesture, she drew him into the living room. "It's that Mars-Saturn aspect."

"Mars? Saturn?" He had a curious feeling he had just left his moorings behind him.

Chapter Three

Come and sit down Mr....McLaughlin.'' Her hand rested lightly on his mud-stained sleeve, and behind her skirts Robin poked her head out like a hand puppet, blond braids swinging, blue eyes batting and a grin like the Cheshire cat on her face.

"You mustn't mind the child—high-spirited Aries. Why don't we have a glass of dandelion wine while we wait for Alison? She's having a bit of trouble with our two tom-cats. Actually they aren't ours." With a dramatic sigh she drew him further into the room. "Perhaps you're not a drinking man. Would herbal tea be more to your liking?"

"The wine will be fine," he replied with amusement.

"Splendid! Please have a seat by the fire, and let me take this." Quickly relieving him of his hand-tailored coat, she muttered, "Well, at least it's dark material. I expect Dog's paw prints will brush off...eventually." Reverently she hung it on an antique coatrack by the door, and with a nod of approval at Blake, she added, "It's good to see a gentleman who dresses."

Blake fingered his navy-and-gold tie. "It's a bit nippy out not to."

"Oh! What I mean to say is—" her hands twirled in the air as if conjuring spirits "—full regalia—suit, tie, et cetera, et cetera." In a voice suggestive of one about to burst into song, she merely pirouetted in a swirl of pink chiffon, headed for the bookshelves that surrounded the fireplace, pushed a panel and withdrew a crystal decanter of pale wine.

"The secret to this wine is to keep it from the light."

"I'll remember that," he assured her solemnly, accepting the brimming goblet.

"Ask him what his sign is!" Robin said, suddenly popping into view, her arms filled with mewing kittens.

"We mustn't rush things, child. Now go and put the kittens down and call your brothers for dinner. Run along and show Mr. McLaughlin what an obedient girl you are."

Undoubtedly Robin had gone to obedience school with Dog, for she held her ground in a similar fashion.

"You know," the child commented at last, "whatever a big cheese is, you're very nice." A dimpled smile designed to melt the coldest heart erupted on her freckled face before she scooted from the room.

"I can't imagine where she learns such language." Blake was certain if Marge owned a fan, she would have used it.

"By the way, Mr. McLaughlin, what sign *are* you?"

"Sign? Oh, you mean when was I born?"

"Yes," she drawled expectantly. "I sense Scorpio." Rapidly she added, "Of course that could be your rising sign hiding your true nature."

"Which is?" he asked on a laugh. If he could just keep her talking, he could find a plant for the god-awful wine.

He smiled above the rim and took a biting sip. Visions of *Arsenic and Old Lace* flitted through his head.

"Ah, well, now that's the mystery. Why, you could even be a closet Virgo, but from what Alison tells me, I doubt that."

"Virgo, the Virgin."

"So you do know a little about it." With a flourish of her bejeweled hand, she tacked on, "You wear your mask well, and I sense you've been through a great deal in your turbulent life." She paused again as her eyes narrowed and a knowing smile slipped across her face. "Perhaps too well, which is not such a good thing."

"Do you send a remittance for your services?" His lips quivered with the hint of a smile, but she dismissed it.

"Definitely Scorpio. Eighth house: other people's money, sex, death and rebirth." She rattled them off with the accomplished ease of an auctioneer, then in another choreographed pivot, headed for a rather exotic whatnot. It was a black medieval piece suggestive of Edgar Allan Poe, and it fitted perfectly in the room. While she fumbled with a lock to one of its drawers, Blake nourished a large rubber plant with dandelion wine. With considerable relief, he settled onto a Victorian love seat.

"My ephemeris!" Marge announced, descending on him like a bat on radar. "Now then, the date and time of your birth?" Her eyebrows rose expectantly above butterfly glasses. She reminded him of Billie Burke playing Glinda the Good in *The Wizard of Oz*. No wonder he liked her.

"November 13, 1944. Sunrise," he answered after a pause.

"Oh, splendid! Scorpio, as I suspected, and thirteen is a very powerful number, as I'm sure you realize." Hastily she thumbed through the small black book. "Ah, yes.

Here you are." Incredible eyelashes fluttered. "My, my! Mars in conjunction with the sun. Nothing—I repeat nothing—stands in your way! Mmm..." She looked at him as if calculating something. Referring back to her source, she said, "The Libra moon should help a little."

"Only a little?" he said on a laugh.

"Oh, I am sure there are other blessings in your chart! Of course, I also think it helps to have a good look at my client's palms. Not that you're a client." Her hand reached for his with the solicitous impersonality of a well-trained physician.

He awaited her verdict with a shadow of a smile on his face. He usually didn't like people to figure him out. Somehow Alison's mother was different, though for the life of him, he couldn't say why. Perhaps it was just her bizarre flamboyance that amused him.

"Now, here's the key." She traced a line on his broad palm and made a soft clucking sound but didn't look at him.

Blake was about to ask for the prognosis when a screeching sound rent the air.

"That will be Studs and Playboy," Marge commented, releasing his hand and looking to the door. Another howl seemed to confirm it. This was followed by a clatter of pots and pans, then a moment of silence before the two cats streaked through the living room and disappeared out the cat door.

"*Pete!* Eric!" Alison yelled at the top of her lungs as she stopped in the doorway. "I just don't know if I can take much more," she mumbled to herself. Then seeing Blake, she said, "Oh! Hello." She gave a futile pat to her lopsided chignon and stepped into the room.

Blake moved to meet her as he responded, "And hello to you." He'd come on business, had encountered bedlam and been astro-analyzed. But all that fell away as he lost himself in the cool depths of her deep green eyes. He felt himself tighten like a coiled spring about to unwind. Everytime he saw her, she seemed more attractive, and Blake had seen quite a few beautiful women. The spell was interrupted as she drew away from his gaze, mumbled something about cats and headed for the front door.

Marge threw her head back and laughed. "You'll have to excuse this chaos, Mr. McLaughlin. By the way, do you mind terribly if I call you Blake?"

"Not at all."

"Well, Blake, if you're going to come around to see Alison, you'll simply have to get used to it—the chaos, I mean. Sometimes I think she even forgets which are her children. So many little ragamuffins running around. But then she does entirely too much: Brownies, Scouts, PTA, her business. Then there's me!" She gave him a wink. "But someone had to take care of the children after Harry died, that is, if Alison's business was going to get off the ground. It was quite a struggle, but she's really doing remarkably well now."

The front door opened on a blast of cold air that ushered in Alison, Pete and Eric. "Now keep those two separated!"

"Right, Mom," the boys chorused as they trudged up the stairs with the bristling cats. Robin brushed past them as she came down.

"I'm getting awfully hungry," she announced for anyone to hear.

"Yes, my precious," Marge trilled. "We're having tofu stew, grain-burgers and, for dessert, a special treat—carob mousse!" Turning to Blake, she added, "It's so important what children eat. In fact, all of us. Then we've always eaten well, and I must say my daughters are radiant examples of vegetarianism. Set the table, Robin. Pete, get Mr. McLaughlin's coat.''

She took a deep breath, preparatory to another discourse, but Alison, who was slipping into her red wool cape, interrupted with, ''Don't wait up. We're discussing business.'' Flashing a professional look in Blake's direction, she started for the door.

Arctic air slammed into them as they made a dash for Blake's car, a vintage Jaguar sedan with running boards, leather seats and a mahogany dash. She thought with some chagrin of her rattletrap station wagon. ''Brrr,'' she said out loud.

''We'll have heat in a minute,'' he replied, easing into first gear. With a crunch of wheels, he maneuvered over the snow. ''I thought you might enjoy dinner at Leonardo's. You been there?''

''Not recently. I've been pretty busy. In fact, I don't usually mix business with pleasure.''

''Ah,'' he countered with a smile. ''But I do.''

Twenty minutes later they were comfortably ensconced at Leonardo's, a small but chic restaurant that catered to the rich and sometimes famous.

''I recommend the vegetarian marinara and the antipasto.'' His dark eyes scanned the menu, ''And their cannelloni rivals the best in Little Italy.''

''I'm game, if you are.''

''Would your mama approve of such rich fare?''

''I *am* over twenty-one, and I don't report home.'' She closed the menu. Looking up at Blake, she was startled by her sudden intake of breath. Nervously she reached for the wine list and, propping it in front of her, made a study of the various wines.

''I think a '75 red would be a good choice,'' he advised in a voice as smooth as the wine was reputed to be. Then with a small gesture, he summoned the waiter and placed their order.

"It's a lovely restaurant," Alison remarked, gazing at the softly lit tables with their snowy cloths and carnation centerpieces. Understated elegance came to mind. "And the food smells delicious." She wrinkled her nose in appreciation.

"I'm glad you like Italian food." He gave her a lazy smile, allowing his gaze to rest on the outline of her breasts as they pressed against the green angora sweater.

She felt the color rise to her cheeks again as he nodded his approval. Why couldn't she have worn something a little less revealing? In a slightly shaky voice, she said, "Please stop looking at me as if... as if..."

"As if you really were Cotton Candi!" he supplied with maddening ease. He leaned back as the waiter appeared with the wine. After tasting it, Blake nodded his satisfaction, raised his glass and murmured, "To you."

Feeling a wave of irritation, she took a bracing sip of dry wine. With exaggerated precision she placed the glass before her. "I am *not* Cotton Candi," she reminded him in a dangerously quiet voice.

"I hadn't forgotten. Good wine, don't you agree?"

"Yes," she clipped out, and to prove it took another sip. It *was* a good year, and a potent one. Already she felt tingly and a little light-headed. Was it from the wine or from the way Blake was gazing at her? No man had ever looked at her quite like that. It made her feel warm—too warm. Abruptly she took another healthy swallow of wine and said, with a try at nonchalance, "Tell me about the Valentino's project. I'm curious why you decided not to sell."

"I had intended to. Then I realized that if Camelot changed the concept and design but kept the name, it would do very well as a ladies' lingerie shop. Demographic studies of the Valentino's locations in various cities show quite a few to be in neighborhoods that are coming up. Popular with the young executive types. And the New Orleans and Georgetown stores couldn't be in a better location.''

Alison made a study of the wineglass before her. Slowly her gaze traveled back to Blake's face. His eyes, lit with a challenging fire, had narrowed and were making a slow appraisal of her.

''Well, I've given it some consideration,'' she said at length in a controlled voice that was at odds with the tingling feelings racing through her. ''Valentino's just isn't in my line.''

''Maybe it should be.'' He poured more wine into her glass. ''Because you know what I think? You're afraid of what Valentino's stands for, aren't you?''

''Nonsense! I'm a grown woman!''

''Yes, I know, with a lot to keep you busy. Could your hesitancy to take on this job be due to prudery? That perhaps—''

''Oh, so now you're going to psychoanalyze me!'' She pressed her lips into a fine line to keep from saying more.

''Perhaps,'' he continued, his eyes brimming with devilishness, ''you're not up to the job because of this aversion to—''

''I assure you, I'm up to any job,'' she snapped with a predictability that annoyed her. ''I'm simply not interested in Valentino's.''

''Maybe you simply can't handle it,'' he repeated offhandedly.

''You play dirty pool, McLaughlin,'' Alison said, ''but you're on! I'll redesign your darling Valentino's so fast it'll

make your head spin! One condition, that I have carte
blanche."

He raised a questioning eyebrow. "Carte blanche?"

"Yes. You either trust me, or you don't. Well?"

"I suppose the red swing will have to go," he said in
deepest mourning.

"Among other things." Twirling the wineglass in her
hand, she added, "You really think this sow's ear can be
changed into a silk purse?"

He brightened immediately. "With your talent we'll
perform miracles. The silk purse I propose will be a pricey
ladies' lingerie shop."

"So, you want something tony, chic and terribly respectable."

"With just a hint of the risqué, supplied nicely by the
name."

"No, the name has to go, too. What we want is something..." She knitted her brows together as if solving a
crime. "Something alluring. Suggestive."

"What can be more suggestive than Valentino's Pleasure?" Blake persisted. "That is, unless you have something against pleasure."

Ignoring this comment, Alison exclaimed, "I have it!
My Lady's Chamber." Her eyes danced with excitement.
"What do you think?"

"You have carte blanche." He gave a maddening shrug
only to add with equal enthusiasm, "You're on!" His
mouth curved into a devastating male grin. "Draw it out.
Scribble it on paper. Whatever you do, do it!"

"I don't scribble things," she said with politeness. "I'm
a designer."

"That's why I'm hiring you. I also think that beneath
that efficient facade lurks a woman who craves beauty and
luxury in her life. The type of woman My Lady's Cham-

ber will cater to. Or don't silk negligees appeal to you?''
There was a hungry look in his eyes, one that Alison
couldn't ignore.

"Tell me something," she managed in a brisk tone. "Do
you usually pick up strangers' business cards when hiring
people?"

Blake leaned back as the waiter appeared with the antipasto. "Let's say, this was a first...for both of us, I trust.
And I've a feeling things are going to turn out quite
nicely." He paused before adding, "I *will* leave it in your
hands. Naturally I'd like to see renderings and so forth,
and to keep in close contact." The look in his eyes suggested much more as he leisurely fingered a marinated
pepper.

"How many stores did you say we were redesigning?"
She gave him her most professional look and hoped he
didn't notice the slight tremble in her voice.

"I didn't, but it's seven altogether. They are the ones in
the workable neighborhoods; we'll close the others. I
thought we might take a look at the Georgetown store tomorrow morning if it's convenient with you."

"Ten o'clock would be fine," she replied in a businesslike tone. Drawing her eyes from his, she made a study of
her antipasto plate. She found his gaze suddenly disconcerting. "Blake," she began hesitantly. "This *is* a business meeting."

"Do I need reminding?" he queried in a teasing tone. "I
didn't think I was out of line, though perhaps my thoughts
were. Perhaps you have your mother's talent for reading
minds."

"It's simply that I sense in you, well, to put it frankly,
you're thinking of me like any other woman."

"Hardly that." He seemed genuinely amused.

"I just want to get the record straight. We're doing business together, and being a woman doesn't alter things." Not much it doesn't! She mentally contradicted her own words. Her pulse was racing. Damn! The way he was looking at her made her feel she was being zapped by a laser beam.

"Being a woman changes a great many things." His voice went straight through Alison. "Is it such a shock for a healthy man to find you attractive? Last night, when I thought you married to some incredibly lucky man, I pulled back. However, now that I see the picture more clearly, I feel we should enjoy our close association."

"Mr. McLaughlin—"

"Oh, we're back to that?" His voice rippled with laughter.

"Considering your intentions—"

"I haven't stated them yet. We're still nibbling on the antipasto. You're a bit of an enigma, Alison, and you do keep a man guessing." He pushed the empty antipasto plate to one side. "Satisfy my curiosity. Why did you lead me to believe your husband was still alive?" His look was expectant.

"Well...I..." Nervously she fingered her gold band.

"You said that he died five years ago."

"Yes, that's true, and, despite what you may think, I really am living in the present, Mr. Mc—Blake," she caught herself and laughed.

"You have a beautiful laugh. It's like a bell." He reached out and touched the side of her face. Instinctively she pulled back. It felt like a whisper of silk against her cheek, igniting all her senses. She hadn't felt like this since her marriage. It was insanity, yet everything else receded into the background.

The spell was interrupted as the waiter announced, "Vegetarian marinara?" and, after placing steaming platters of noodles before them, sang out *"Mangia bene"* as an exit note.

"Mangia bene," Blake echoed, his voice light, almost teasing. Refilling their wineglasses, he said, "Here's to a long and prosperous partnership, with all the fringe benefits."

"We can leave off the benefits," she quickly corrected, wondering if the flush in her cheeks was still evident. Then in a stronger voice, she added, "Strictly business, Blake. I mean it."

"So do I." The teasing look in his eyes sent another shiver of unwanted longing through her. She would not play into his hands. Yes, he was attractive, but there were a lot of attractive men in the world, and she wasn't looking for one, despite the needs he seemed to resurrect in her.

Turning her attention to the dinner, she noted the marinara was cooked to perfection. The sauce was an aromatic delight, and the salad and hot bread that accompanied it were delicious.

The meal almost succeeded in taking Alison's mind off Blake's intentions, which she was sure were far from honorable. With the arrival of the luscious cannelloni, Alison was feeling both sated and relaxed. She should have known better.

"Let me guess what you do first thing in the morning," he remarked softly after coffee had been served. Pinning her with one of his practiced looks, he drawled, "You take a few laps around your indoor pool—"

"I don't have a pool, indoor or outdoor." She leveled a cool glance at him. The tone of his voice spoke volumes.

"Well, there are other early-morning exercises," he offered, "Perhaps you'd care for lessons."

"Thank you, but no," she countered.

He gave her a dazzling smile. "You can't fault me for trying, can you?"

"No, I suppose not." She laughed in spite of herself. "I guess you could say we both stand forewarned."

"Pretty evenly matched," he commented, and signaled for the check. "It has been a most enjoyable evening. I look forward to many more during the course of Valentino's transformation into My Lady's Chamber."

"You seem to forget I'm going to do this in record time," Alison declared with satisfaction.

"Would you care to make a wager on that?"

"A wager?"

"Yes. You know, betting? You look like a gamblin' woman to me."

"Don't bet on it," she managed. She leaned back in her chair and gave him an appraising look of her own. So, this man thought he had all the answers; she'd see about that. Certainly the faster she got the job done, the sooner he'd get out of her life. "Three weeks and you've got yourself a starting point for contractors." She watched him sign for the check and slip his gold card back into his wallet.

"What are the stakes?" he asked in a voice so silky it sent another flurry of unwanted desire though her. Damn the man. He could turn on seduction like some people do their radios. And Alison had a feeling his wiring was all in the right place and *very* hot. She could just imagine what kind of stakes he'd like to put up. He exuded power and winning, and she had a feeling he was not one for unwise speculation.

"Then again, perhaps you'd like to think about it." He had risen swiftly to his feet. Crossing behind her chair, he bent down and whispered in her ear, "I'm sure something of significance will come to mind."

The aura of masculinity he wrapped around her practically rendered her speechless. She was suddenly all too aware of her pounding heartbeat. Were those his hands resting on her shoulders? she wondered. Squeezing ever so gently, they sent a thousand prickles down her arms and deeper still. She had the ridiculous feeling he had just claimed her—branded her as his. With this fleeting thought, she felt him step back, but the bond, like invisible thread, was still there between them.

She tried reminding herself that things like this just didn't happen. Especially not to sensible people like Alison O'Shaunnessey Sherwood. She smiled what she felt must have been a ridiculous smile. At least she wasn't babbling the way some women did when they got nervous. But why was she nervous? Because this very handsome man looked as though he could eat her!

Somewhere deep inside, Alison feared that her love was a jinx. It was a ridiculous thought, but it had been with her for a long time. Don't love this man, an inner voice told her. Nothing good will come of it. A flash of memory and she was there again, in front of the TV, staring stupidly as the wreckage of Harry's Pinto, sideswiped on the Beltway by an eighteen-wheeler, appeared on the news. Her grief had healed, but not the fear.

They rode home through the snowy Georgetown streets in silence, but when they came to a red light at Wisconsin and Que Streets, he smoothly slid his arm around her. Before she could protest, he leaned over and brushed his lips against hers, tentatively, savoring their flavor, then claiming her mouth in a deep kiss that seemed to go on forever. A yielding fire leaped within her, but a warning bell in her head sounded. She pulled away and found her voice. "Please, don't do that again."

"I can't promise," he said huskily. Leaning back, he looked at her in a way that left her breathless. With a charming, unexpected grin, he added, "Rest assured, my intentions are good. It's just that you've bewitched me."

"I'm sure," she replied after a moment. Recklessly she tacked on, "Like the other women in your life."

"You mustn't believe the press! It's not as though I have a stable. Don't you believe in a little pleasure in your life? If not, you'd have fooled me."

"Let's just say I don't enjoy being chased for a one-night stand." She clamped her mouth shut and stared straight ahead. She'd said too much as it was.

"Did I say 'one-night stand'?" As the light changed, he skidded forward and grumbled, "Damn Georgetown streets, why can't they put some salt down?" After a moment he gave her a wary look. "Just because I don't get emotionally involved with every woman I date doesn't mean I have one-nighters and dump women. It isn't that simple, Alison."

She wanted to protest, but the feel of his kiss was still on her lips, vibrating and shattering her senses.

"However," he continued, "let's get back to your wager." She knew from the smooth sound of his voice that he was smiling. "Three weeks, is it? And if you forfeit?"

"Don't be ridiculous, Blake McLaughlin." Though she was still a little shaky, she was beginning to feel more normal. "I won't lose! Besides, there are no family jewels left."

"Oh? I beg to differ."

Outside, sleet pinged against the windshield. Blake was challenging Alison's world and luring her deeper and deeper into unknown territory—to the place where her heart was, guarded from just such intrusions.

He walked her to the front door with the caution of one navigating a minefield. Satisfied that all was safe, he kissed her on the forehead and whispered, ''You have emerald eyes, that's jewel enough for me.'' Turning, he left, taking great care as he went down the steps.

Emeralds. She mouthed the word as she picked up Pete's skateboard. It was a wonder someone hadn't been killed the way her kids littered the porch. She'd have to get on them about it in the morning.

Her cheeks tingled for the umpteenth time that evening, and for a brief moment she wondered what it would be like to have him seduce her.

''Emeralds,'' she repeated out loud. Then a memory, like the jewel itself, brightened at the end of a tunnel of time. Long ago her father had called her ''emerald eyes.''

Chapter Four

It took all of Alison's willpower to drag herself from bed and head for the shower. Thank God she had her own bathroom. When she'd first married Harry, it was the only thing they disagreed on. He'd believed in family living. He'd grown up with four brothers, and they'd managed nicely with one bathroom. Alison said, no, they would have at least two. Since Harry had been a fairly well-off attorney, they'd settled on two and a half bathrooms, and he'd jokingly contended it kept their marriage together.

Down the hall she could hear the boys fighting in the other bathroom. Robin was pounding on the door, demanding her turn, and Dog was barking. Turning the shower jets on full blast, Alison managed to drown out the ruckus. She'd definitely stayed up too late last night. It was one of her worse faults. She enjoyed puttering around or reading before going to sleep. Last night she had been particularly worked up. She'd toyed with the idea of backing off the Valentino's job, shelved the notion, then fixed herself a huge bowl of popcorn and settled in bed with an Agatha Christie. That behavior was not conducive to her seven o'clock jog.

She stepped from the steamy shower, dried off, dressed in sweatpants and a top, and headed down the stairs. As usual Marge was up, and a delicious aroma of waffles filled the air. Too bad she had eaten all that popcorn.

Alison stopped dead in her tracks as Blake McLaughlin entered the dining room from the kitchen, laden down with several dishes. He sent a maddening smile in her direction and casually remarked, "My curiosity got the better of me."

"Your curiosity?" She blinked twice and slowly walked toward him. He was setting *her* table, for God's sake!

"You said you didn't have a pool, but I knew a girl with an appetite like yours must do something to stay so—" his dark eyes roved appreciatively over her "—fit. I don't think olive green's your color, though."

"I don't give a damn what you think." She circled the table toward him. "You mean this impromptu visit is due to idle curiosity about my morning habits?"

"In part. I was also wondering what Marge would serve for breakfast, being as she disapproves of bacon."

"You really take the cake, you know that?"

"No, it's waffles with rice syrup, tempeh bacon and grain coffee. Quite good, actually, that is if you don't think of all those poor soybeans sacrificing their lives for a strip of fake bacon." His mouth curved in another of his annoying smiles. Alison scowled back and started for the kitchen. "You know, Ms. Sherwood," he called after her in mock solemnity, "I don't think mornings are your best time."

"Mother," Alison began, as she reached behind a tin of brewer's yeast for her stash of real coffee. "How long has Mr. McLaughlin been here?"

"Oh, is it 'mister' now?" Marge asked as she pried open the waffle iron. On a disappointed note, she added, "Alison! You know how caffeine affects you."

"Exactly. That's why I'm having two cups. Maybe I'll get reckless and have three...with sugar," she declared wickedly.

"We don't have any of that poison in the house, and you know it." Marge sniffed as she flipped the fake bacon onto a napkin.

"Dunk Me Donuts does." Alison rapped her nails on the tabletop, waiting for the hot water to come to a boil.

"Oh, there you are!" Marge cried out as Blake appeared. "Everything's just about ready, and the kids will be down in a minute. If you don't mind putting this on—" she shoved a platter of waffles and a pot of coffee in his direction "—I'll tend to this last waffle."

"Delighted," Blake muttered as he backed his way out the swinging door.

"Such a gentleman." Marge clucked as she gave her curls a pat. She was dressed in her morning clothes, a frilly gingham apron over a hot-pink pantsuit. Her face was fully made-up, lacking only the turquoise eye shadow, which was reserved for the evening hours.

"Well, I'm off for my jog," Alison announced as she poured boiling water over the coffee.

"Mind if I join you?" Blake asked as he reappeared.

"Wearing that?" Without waiting for an answer, Alison brushed past him and headed for the door.

"Thought I'd drive my car alongside you."

"You really would, wouldn't you?" Shrugging her shoulders, she consulted her watch. "Suit yourself, but wouldn't you rather stick around for breakfast?"

"Nope." He was leaning against the front door, looking sexier than he had a right to. Maybe it was the clothes, Alison thought as she took in the three-piece dark wool suit, burgundy tie and crisp white shirt, all tailor-made and undoubtedly expensive. He looked the part of a wealthy executive who was equally at home in both boardroom and bedroom.

"Your breakfast will be cold when you get back," she said, exiting. "And so will you."

"I'm driving, remember? Next time, I'll come dressed for the occasion."

Alison whirled around. "Our working together does not extend to breakfast." Her breath frosted before her, and she automatically began to jog in place.

"Marge said she'd love to have me." Giving her a pat on the cheek, he opened his car door and lowered himself onto the seat. "You see, I'm just irresistible to women of all ages."

"What you are, Mr. McLaughlin, is terribly conceited, and if it weren't for all that filthy lucre you are going to pay me, I'd tell you to go sit on a tack!" A smile sprang to her lips in spite of everything. She would jog it off, she assured herself. Lord, it was cold.

"You know," he called out the car window as he turned on the ignition and began a snail's pace alongside her, "we could take a long lunch hour and jog at my gym."

"Your gym?" she echoed back.

"Yes. You know, you shouldn't jog in all this traffic."

"What traffic? Tulip Lane is practically a country road. Well, it will be in a minute," she amended as she stopped for a red light, jogging in place as cars sped by. Then, cocking her head in his direction, she said, "This is the most ridiculous way to have a conversation. I can't imagine what you're getting out of it." She shrugged her shoulders and headed across the street.

What I'm getting out of it, he thought, as he cruised behind the irrepressible Alison Sherwood, is incredible. Just looking at her in that awful olive-green sweat suit made him feel like a high school kid on his first date with a real hot tamale, as they used to call them. Maybe that was part of the curse of growing up in the fifties, hitting puberty in the sixties and middle age in the eighties. Until his wife died, he'd always kept women on a pedestal. The heartache had finally eased, but his quest for the ideal woman—one to replace Ginny—hadn't. There had been a series of affairs that had about as much punch as a flat, warm beer. There had been one or two champagnes, but none to match Alison. And *none* of the women he'd known would have been caught in the outfit she so proudly sported. Ginny had been like that, too. A free spirit...

Shaking himself from these thoughts, Blake noticed her country lane was about to turn into a gravel footpath that cut through the Monthaven Estate. He'd been up there once or twice when the kids were little, but lately he'd been too busy. He remembered Sondra liked it because the house there reminded her of Tara in *Gone with the Wind*. Up ahead he could see that Alison was slowing down. They were on an uphill stretch that wound into a tunnel of boxwood. He'd have to park the car because the road ended. Slowing down considerably, he gazed at the snowy mounds where the plow truck had cleared a path. The sky was the color of a sapphire, not a cloud in sight. But the air was snapping cold.

"Hold up," he called out as he parked the car in a small space provided for those wishing to continue on foot. "I'll join you."

"Aren't you afraid of getting your shoes all snowy?" Her voice had a teasing, becoming lilt to it. Jogging obviously improved her spirits.

"A little snow won't hurt them."

"I thought you preferred the indoor track." The jauntiness was still in her voice. She squinted up at him, one hand shielding her eyes against the morning sun, the other casually anchored at her hip.

"I'll take any track I can get," he remarked as he matched his pace to hers.

"I slow down on this part of the run." She gave a panting laugh. "It's all uphill, but aren't the boxwood beautiful?"

"Spectacular," he mumbled. She was right, it was ridiculous having a conversation while jogging uphill in twenty-degree weather.

She slowed down and grabbed at her sides. "Let's walk for a minute."

He could hear her breathing hard and fast. Out of the corner of his eye he saw her rosy cheeks and that adorable profile with its turned-up nose. He wanted nothing more than to crush her in his arms—and get her out of that wretched green sweat suit!

"See up ahead? That's Monthaven. They say an English earl bought it before the Civil War as a wedding gift for his bride. He worshiped the ground she walked on, that is, until he found her in the arms of the stable boy. He killed them both and threw their bodies in the Potomac River. Then he slashed her portrait and shot himself—right there in the parlor. The estate stood vacant for years—haunted so they say. Finally, Harvard University acquired it, and it's now a museum.'' She faced him, and he noticed her eyes were sparkling. "Everything's just as it was in 1860. It's really remarkable.''

"Sounds as if it made quite an impression on you.''

"Inspired me to become a decorator.''

"I suppose that explains your aversion to whips and chains and garish pink flamingos.''

"Undoubtedly.'' She threw her head back and laughed. It sounded like silver bells to Blake McLaughlin. He shook his head as if to dislodge such a fanciful thought.

"You've been inside?'' she asked after a moment as they neared the crest of the hill.

"A few years back my daughter insisted we come. I think women like this sort of place. Maybe it fulfills their Prince Charming fantasy.''

"There's nothing wrong with that,'' she shot back good-humoredly.

"Except that it sets you up for disappointment.'' He was tempted to add more, but maybe certain things were better left unsaid.

Alison chose to ignore his remark and went on cheerily, "I thought you just had the one child. You know, the trumpet player?''

"He has an older sister, Sondra. She's fourteen going on twenty-one.'' His own harsh laughter caught him off guard. He didn't want to discuss his daughter, nor his obvious inadequacies as a parent, especially not with Alison.

"Does she live with you?'' Alison gently asked as they paused at the top of the hill.

"Yes.'' His voice tripped over the word as if it were foreign. His gaze slipped from hers, but not before she'd seen the flash of pain. His eyes searched the crest of the hill, and in an even quieter voice, he said, "My wife, Ginny, died three years ago.'' His lips tightened against the emotion. "She was a wonderful woman . . . and her death was particularly hard on Sondra."

"I'm so sorry," Alison said, at a loss for words yet feeling this man's grief. "I imagine its been hard on you, too."

Raw honesty swept his face, stripping the mask there, raising the veil for an instant. "I was a madman when the doctor came out of the operating room. They said they'd done everything they could to save her. I don't even remember those first six months after she was gone. I sort of walked around in a haze, on automatic. I had my work, but as a parent I was pretty lousy. I kept thinking that if I could find someone like Ginny again, the kids would have a mother and I would have—" He cut himself off. No point in telling Alison that there was something about her that reminded him of Ginny. "Sondra was eleven at the time." He turned slowly and started down the hill. The only sounds were the crunch of shoes on snow and the far-off purr of traffic.

"I'd like to meet your daughter sometime," Alison tactfully suggested, catching up with him.

"She's a bit of a problem," Blake confessed.

"It's probably not that bad. Fourteen is a difficult age."

"I honestly don't see much improvement ahead." They had reached the car, and opening the door, he said, "But you're welcome to try." He smiled tentatively. "Though I didn't know I was hiring a child counselor, as well as a designer."

"Remember, I'm multifaceted, Mr. McLaughlin!"

"Indeed. May I give you a lift home, Dr. Sherwood, I presume."

"Thank you."

* * *

While Marge made another batch of waffles and more

fake bacon, Alison quickly freshened up and changed into a one-piece red wool dress with a cowl collar and raglan sleeves that made it divinely comfortable. As an added thought she put gold studs in her ears and hung her grandmother's gold watch around her neck. She fashioned her dark hair in its usual topknot and heightened her natural color with blusher and lipstick.

Though it was still early, Payowakit had managed to get sick on the living room carpet, and Dog had succeeded in terrorizing the new domestic with her antics.

"I had to put her in the basement," Marge announced as she brought on hot waffles. "Ramarama Nanda said she was manifesting the discordant ethers in our household. Imagine!"

"Rama *who*?" Alison asked as she poured syrup on her waffles.

"Ra-ma-ra-ma Nanda," Marge said slowly as if instructing a backward child. "She's the domestic who's replacing Hannah this week. Quiet thing, though a bit plump for a follower of Guru Shikti-something-or-other." She waved her hand to indicate his unimportance. "She has a rather yogurty look about her. I understand they live on the stuff."

Blake, who'd been quiet until now, interjected, "I thought you approved of things like yogurt." He had speared a thick slab of fake bacon and was waving it as if it were an indictment.

"Dairy?" Marge's lashes fluttered triple time. "Heaven's no! Nasty stuff that. Did you know that we're the only species who drinks another's milk?" She wrinkled her nose to make her point.

Blake slanted Alison an odd look, as if he'd just discovered she came from another planet. "You mean you grew up without drinking milk?"

Alison nodded. "It's not as if we were fed bread and water, and it's not that big a deal." She chewed thoughtfully on a piece of waffle. "I'm all in one piece."

"Indeed, my girls are beauties," Marge trilled as she hovered over the table. "You see, Blake, when you don't eat meat your system requires less calcium, but tofu and kale and—"

"Mama," Alison interrupted softly, "I think Blake gets the idea." Pushing her plate to one side, she glanced at her watch. "Oh, my goodness! Almost nine o'clock."

"I've got you for the morning, remember?" Blake said, finishing up the last of his waffle.

"I still have to check in with the office, even if I do run it!" Clearing the table, she headed for the kitchen, only to collide with what appeared to be either a fat ghost or a large woman dressed up in a sheet. Plates flew in all directions, coffeepot and syrup smashed to the floor, and the white sheet shrieked in tongues.

"Does she speak English?" Alison asked her mother as she began picking up sticky pieces of plate.

"Of course," Marge remarked testily. "You're late for work, leave that. Ramarama Nanandra and I will clean it up." She made a face at her flustered mispronunciation, and brushing past the quivering white sheet, went into the kitchen.

"It's the spirits," the sheet ruminated, standing stock-still. Only her third chin waggled a little. Alison noted this from her crouched position. Slowly, she rose and looked the woman in the eye.

"Spirits, you say? Well, I'm sure you and my mother will be able to wish them well. Unfortunately, my friend and I have to leave." She turned toward Blake, who seemed to find the scene amusing, and said, "Ready?" Then she spoke to the woman in white. "Have a good day!" This was the domestic who supposedly cleaned parquet floors with a toothbrush? Alison seriously doubted if she could bend over that far.

"Mommy! Mommy!" Robin raced into the room with Dog at her heels. "Look who I found in the basement. And she made a *big* puddle." The child stopped in her tracks. "Who's that in the Halloween costume?"

Dog knew. She yapped for joy and charged at Ramarama Nanda, who teetered against the kitchen door before crashing through. This was a new game for Dog, who looked puzzled but galloped after her.

"Hey, man, what's all the racket?" Pete appeared with his brother Eric in tow. "We were doing great on the computer. I was winning at—" The eldest boy stepped forward. "Mom, you been drinking Granny's dandelion wine or something?"

"Don't get funny, young man. We've just had a little accident." Alison pushed the kitchen door open. Rama Randa, or whatever her name was, had propped herself against the wall and was chanting. Marge was just returning from tying Dog in the backyard. She had an it's-all-in-a-day's-work look on her face. Alison felt warm bodies press against her: Robin, Pete, Eric, maybe even Blake, though she doubted it. He was probably still at the table.

"Run along, all of you!" Marge said as she picked up the broom and dustpan. "School bus will be here any minute."

"Is she all right? Rama-mama, are you okay?" Alison addressed her directly and received an affirmative nod for her pains.

"Is that one of Granny's friends?" Pete ventured, poking his freckled face into the kitchen.

"Probably been at the dandelion wine," Eric offered with a snicker. At ten, he was the next to oldest and going through a lamentable "toughie" stage.

Alison whirled around, assumed her drill sergeant role and yelled, "Out, all of you!"

"Heck," Eric grumbled. "Won't even give your kids a kiss, much less lunch! We're *de*-prived!"

"Kiss?" Pete mocked, "What's this kiss routine?" He gave his brother a shove. "We could use some grub, though."

Too much television, Alison thought distractedly as she ran her fingers though her hair. "Your lunch boxes are by the front door like they always are."

"Mommy, what about the puddle in the basement?" Robin asked. "It's real big."

"I'll take care of it." The school bus honked its horn, and Alison sighed in relief. "Now, all you scoot." She bent down and gave Robin the expected kiss.

The little girl paused, then blurted out, "Pete watched a *Gunsmoke* rerun last night!" She stuck her tongue out at him and said, "I didn't want to look at your old comic books anyway!"

"You know that Rama-Mama might be right," Blake said as he held the door to Valentino's for Alison.

"About what?" Alison asked, blinking her eyes in an attempt to adjust to the pulsating black light.

"Spirits," he whispered in solemn tones. "Things that go bump in the night."

"Ha! And in the morning, too. This lighting scheme has to go! If possible, it's worse than New Orleans." She grimaced at a particularly dreadful display: a life-size poster of James Dean flanked by fluorescent pink flamingos. She pressed her lips into a flat line as a slim-hipped punk slithered toward them. He made Pink Glitter look tame in comparison. Stiletto hair sprang like bone from his gaunt face. His penciled eyebrows emphasized the Joan Crawford look which he'd adapted right down to the padded forties print jacket. Handcuffs dangled from a chain belt, and patched jeans completed the ensemble.

"Somethin' I can do fer you?" He spoke from the side of his mouth, gangster style.

Blake withdrew his card, placed it on the counter and said, "I'm the new owner, Blake McLaughlin, and this is my designer, Ms. Sherwood. We just want to look around."

"Fer sure," the punk with the Crawford jacket mumbled. "Guess you'll be making big changes around here." Without waiting for an answer, he sauntered off, Blake's card stuck between his teeth like a tasty toothpick.

"Big changes," Alison emphasized as she looked around. "I'll need a floor plan of the shop."

"You'll have it this afternoon."

"You really mean what you said last night?" Lest he misunderstand, she quickly tacked on, "About my having carte blanche."

"Would I lead you on?" His mouth twitched in amusement as he added, "See anything here that turns you on? Aside from yours truly?"

"I've seen enough," she replied breezily. In a crisp and authoritative voice, one that hopefully masked her inner tension, she said, "As soon as I get those floor plans, I'll start to work."

"And have it completed in—what was it? Three weeks?" He stared at her through shuttered eyes, and for that one moment Alison was reminded of a sleek and hungry predator, a jungle beast that waited, then pounced at the least likely time.

"I made a wager and I stand by it."

"I like a betting woman," he said softly.

Another, louder, song burst full blast over the speakers. Blake claimed her arm and steered her toward the door as he said, "Why don't you come over to my office. We can have some coffee while I dig up those floor plans."

"Thanks, but I'll take a rain check on it. I've really got to get back to *my* office." They had reached their cars and Alison was jangling her keys, preparatory to leaving.

"Does the place fall apart without you?"

"Never can tell." She quickly opened the car, tossed her briefcase on the front seat and climbed in. Blake leaned in the window until his mouth was only a breath away from hers. She felt an unwanted shiver of pleasure inch up her spine. "I have to go now," she said hoarsely.

"Then I'll call as soon as I have the plans, and perhaps we can meet later."

"Perhaps," she managed to reply in a steady voice. "Or you could send them by courier as I'm sure you have a busy day, too."

"I'll just have to rearrange my priorities and put you at the top of the list." His voice was a warm caress on a very cold day, and the look he sent her brooked no interference. "I've been told I have a stubborn streak," he added.

"That's an understatement! In fact, I think you fibbed when you told Mama you were a Scorpio!"

"Oh?" He seemed amused at this accusation.

"Taurus the bull suits you much better." With a self-satisfied smile, she gunned the engine and said, "Unless you want to lose your toes, you'll step back."

"Until later, Ms. Sherwood." His dark eyes sparkled with something unspoken, and he stepped back onto the curb.

Alison gripped the steering wheel and managed to pull out of the parking space. Her heart had started that ridiculous pounding again, all because of a man who refused to play by the rules. A man who broke the rules, and, unless Alison was very much mistaken, a man who could break her heart.

"Damn," she muttered to herself. "Oh, double damn!"

Chapter Five

The afternoon was a total waste for Blake. After locating the Georgetown floor plans for Alison, he attempted to dictate several letters to McGee, but finally gave up and told his secretary to take the rest of the day off. She in turn suggested that perhaps it was he who needed the rest, and was he feeling well? Perhaps, some chicken soup? When she pulled out her thermometer, he gently showed her the door.

"Tomorrow, Edith. Go to Neiman's and buy a dress."

She sniffed, "I never shop there. Only Garfinckels." Sheathing the thermometer and stuffing it back into her purse, she scurried down the corridor. He knew she was thinking that he was headed for an early grave or, as she colorfully put it "on the express train for hell." At least once a month she surreptitiously slipped articles under his door: "Are You Type A?" or "Workaholics Anonymous." What is it about me that attracts the mothering type? he wondered. Undoubtedly a lack in his childhood.

He chuckled at the heyday Edith and Marge would have if they met. The carnivore and the vegetarian locking horns. McGee believed there was nothing chicken soup or a good porterhouse steak couldn't cure.

Alison O'Shaunnessey Sherwood. He repeated the name silently, then abruptly crossed to the curved bank of windows and stared out at the Washington skyline barely visible through a bank of thick snow clouds. In another hour it would be dark, cold and probably snowing. But in another hour he and Alison would be having a cocktail, discussing Valentino's and getting to know each other better. He held off calling her, not wanting to seem overly eager. The irony was that he was overly eager, which was a first for Blake, who usually had to fend off the admiring women. His popularity had never fazed Ginny, but then she was one of the few women who hadn't been blinded by the money and power, another similarity she and Alison shared.

For whatever reason, this cool attitude on Alison's part merely kept the fires going. He'd call her. Now.

Crossing to the desk, he flipped his Rolodex, found the number and, lifting the receiver, dialed it. It rang four, five, six times. Impatiently he tapped his fingers on the mahogany desk. He was not a man who liked to be kept waiting.

"Alison Sherwood," he barked into the phone on the seventh ring.

"Speaking," was the startled reply. "Blake?"

"Didn't mean to bite your head off, but don't you have anyone on the switchboard?"

"We don't have a switchboard. If one of the assistants can't get it, it rings back to either my desk or Ingrid's."

"You should have one," he countered abruptly.

"That's the reason for this call? Blake, I'm really in a rush."

"I've got the floor plans, and I thought I'd drop them by." He rolled them up and slid them into a tube as he spoke. "We could make happy hour at the Harbor Bar. It's on Thirty-fourth Street near my house." His tone had softened considerably.

She paused before replying, "I'm not much of a drinker."

"Frozen peach daiquiris?"

She laughed. "Margaritas!"

"We're on. How does five-thirty sound?"

"What about your children?"

"Willy's at trumpet practice from five-thirty till seven, and Sondra's fourteen going on twenty-one, remember?"

"Yes." Hesitation edged her voice. "Well, be sure you bring those floor plans."

"I'll have them."

Alison quickly returned the receiver to the cradle as Ingrid came into the room with a knowing smile on her face.

"From your expression I'll bet that was the mysterious Mr. McLaughlin."

"Oh, for heaven's sake, don't go reading anything into it." Alison fussed with papers on her desk to avoid her friend's probing gaze.

"I'm not!" Sidling up to the desk, she irreverently sat on the edge. "Just happy you've taken on the job. I think it's a hoot it's Valentino's!"

"For the fee he's paying, I'd redesign anything." Crossing to her drafting board, she made a pretense of studying a rendering as she carelessly added, "Teal blue would be better than periwinkle for the sitting room, don't you think?"

"Periwinkle is divine," Ingrid enthused. "And so is Mr. McLaughlin."

"You don't really even know him," Alison protested as she pulled out several color samples for inspection.

Ingrid ignored this. "I really do like the periwinkle and so does Mrs. Billings—you know, *our client*."

With a sigh, Alison shoved the samples into the drawer and turned to face Ingrid. "He's just so...so sure of himself. You know the type."

"I like his type, and if you had any sense, so would you. But a word to the wise is sufficient." Ingrid shrugged her shoulders. "Aside from the personal angle, don't forget your Mr. McLaughlin might become a permanent client. I mean he has scads of accounts—big bucks, little Alison, not to mention fringe benefits." She withdrew her car keys from her purse and, jingling them like a bell, added, "I'd love to hang around to meet him, but I promised Ted I'd join him for dinner." Blowing a kiss, she hopped off the desk and left.

Thank God, Alison hadn't told Ingrid her Mr. McLaughlin had shown up for breakfast! With grim determination she withdrew makeup from her purse. Her hand trembled as she applied her burgundy lipstick. It was a business partnership, she went on to remind herself as she rolled on a dark coat of mascara. If he chose to put more into it, so be it! The attraction between them was chemistry, nothing more. Hadn't he implied he made no commitments? Snapping her compact shut, she headed for her desk and a pile of bills.

She had just finished paying the last one when the buzzer sounded. With a sigh, she scraped her chair away from the desk and headed down the narrow flight of stairs to the front door. Everyone had gone home and she'd have to let him in herself.

She started to tell him to come on up, but stared in amazement at the dozen roses that Blake thrust at her.

"Godiva chocolates next time," he said.

Alison sputtered a thank-you, and clasping the American Beauties to her breast, headed back up the stairs. Her heart was beginning to thump double time again. "I'll just get a vase," she said somewhat awkwardly. Gesturing toward the reception area, she added, "Have a seat."

"Thanks," he murmured. Crossing the room, he settled into one of the antique love seats.

"The roses are lovely," Alison called from the kitchen as she hastily ran water into a tall vase. Flowers, cocktails... She didn't want to think of where this evening was leading. When she reentered, he was thumbing through a magazine and looking incredibly handsome. His cashmere coat was unbuttoned. She could see that he'd loosened his tie, and that the vest he'd been sporting that morning was gone.

"They'll look nice on the mantel," she said in a high and slightly nervous voice.

"Do I get an official tour this time?" he asked softly.

Alison turned slowly toward him. "I think you've seen just about everything. This is the reception area, originally it was the master bedroom." Blake raised an amused eyebrow, and she quickly went on, "And right down the hall is the kitchen, which leads to the old dining room, where Ingrid and her assistant work. The living room has been converted to my workroom. This building is quite old, but remarkably functional." She hated the prim sound of the way she said *functional*.

Blake brushed past her and started down the narrow hall. "Remember, I'm a Scorpio, and they're terribly curious," he commented, poking his head into the kitchen. Smiling at her, he added, "Snoops of the zodiac, right?"

Without waiting for a reply, he continued, "I read my horoscope this morning. It said I'm about to win a major victory." He paused at the door to her office. "Remarkable," he muttered. "It's as neat as a pin."

"My Mars is in Virgo, but watch out, I'm a Leo with Aries rising." She flashed him a smile. "And now before we head out for drinks, how about the floor plans?"

"Business before pleasure," he countered, handing her a cardboard tube. "The entire chain has approximately the same layout, give or take a few feet. You know how franchises are."

"I'll have some renderings and estimates by the beginning of next week, as promised, and once you approve, we'll start work." Unfurling the floor plan, she studied it for a few minutes. After making some notations, she rolled it back up and slipped it into the tube. "I might even have this completed in less time than I originally thought."

"Great, and now for those margaritas."

"One will be fine," she tossed back with a grin.

By the time they'd reached the Harbor Bar, Alison was looking forward to that margarita. "I usually just brush the salt off the rim," she said as they entered the dimly lit bar. Frank Sinatra, crooning on an ancient jukebox, was in keeping with the slick World War II decor. Red vinyl booths with Formica-topped tables flanked walls that were covered with wartime posters. A circular brass-trimmed bar was located dead center and filled to capacity with yuppies, college kids and a smattering of in-search-of singles. A woman with shoulder-length auburn hair and too much makeup stared for a moment at Blake, then abruptly swung back to her drink, her hair falling like a curtain, obscuring her features.

Blake tensed. "Wait here," he ordered as he strode toward the bar. Openmouthed, Alison watched as he practically yanked the woman from the stool. Heated words were exchanged as he steered her from the bar. His hand was wrapped firmly around her arm as she frantically tried to get loose. As they approached Alison, she realized this "woman" was a teenager, and most probably Blake's daughter, Sondra. As they stopped before her, the girl was still clawing at her father's hand.

"You like your girlfriends to wear tight clothes! And you bring *them* down here! Besides, I've done my homework." The girl's red mouth drew into a pout as she tossed her auburn hair defiantly. Her actions had the studied look of a daytime soap opera actress.

Blake, his face dark with anger, said, "I'll be back shortly, after I've taken my daughter home. Order me a martini and grab the booth by the window." He indicated with a jerk of his head. "I won't be long. We live just around the corner. Later, when my daughter is in a better frame of mind, I'll introduce you."

"There's nothing wrong with my frame of mind, thank you, Father!" She gave another toss of her head as he led her toward the lobby.

Alison claimed the window booth and numbly looked out on Thirty-fifth Street. What was wrong with the girl? Dressing like that and sitting alone in a bar. For that matter, what was wrong with Blake, chewing his daughter out because she mimicked his girlfriends? Alison felt a wave of irritation hit her. Of course the man had girlfriends, and thankfully Alison was not, nor would she be, one of them! Her thoughts went back to Sondra. Fourteen going on twenty-one, sitting alone in a bar, drinking...what? Cherry cola? Rum and Coke? What else did Sondra McLaughlin do when her father was working late or out on the town or with one of his various lady friends? And did teenage girls really call their fathers "Father" anywhere but in 1930s British movies?

"May I take your order?" a waiter asked.

"A margarita, no salt, and a martini for my friend, who'll be returning in a few minutes."

As the waiter disappeared, Alison's thoughts returned to Blake's daughter. Evidently the death of Sondra's mother *had* keenly affected her, and Blake was understandably unequal to the task of being a single parent. Alison was still mulling this over when Blake and the drinks arrived simultaneously. His eyes were bright and his cheeks were flushed with what she knew was anger. He collapsed in the booth and clenched his hands in front of him.

"Sorry about that," he said. "She's never done anything like that before...to my knowledge." His lips twisted into a wry smile.

"To your knowledge," Alison repeated softly, taking a sip of her margarita.

"I don't know what to do with her," he confessed. "She's not really bad...just..."

"Looking for attention? Or maybe even love?" Alison ran her fingers around the rim of the glass. She'd promised herself she wouldn't get involved, but she had to say something.

He didn't seem to hear her. "I've been thinking about what to do for some time, and tonight confirmed it. I'm sending her to boarding school. Brockingham's in Richmond."

"I don't think that's the answer, Blake. She might feel rejected."

"Listen, she's *my* daughter!" His chin jutted forward and his eyes snapped with intense fire. "After midsemester break-I'm switching schools, and that's that."

Alison leaned forward and quietly said, "You're right, Sondra *is* your daughter, which is why it's so hard for you to make this decision. Have you tried counseling?"

"You sound like Ann Landers!"

"Well, Blake, the child is obviously troubled."

"And I suppose it's my fault." He tasted his martini and made a face.

"I'm sure no one's at fault. These are hard times to raise kids in—look at the handful I've got."

"But no delinquents, is that what you're saying?"

"You've missed the point."

"I suggest we shelve this topic and enjoy our drinks." He raised the martini in a mock toast.

"On one condition, Blake." Her voice was soft, but firm. "That you bring Willy and Sondra to dinner tomorrow night."

"I can't promise they'll go for your mother's soybean soufflé, but I suppose it won't kill them." His good humor was returning, and a ghost of a smile haunted his lips.

"How did you know about her soufflé?" She blinked in surprise across the margarita.

"Marge already invited us."

"Oh!" She took a sip of the drink and placed it carefully on the cocktail napkin. "Mother is quite an extrovert. Then you'll bring them?"

"Yes. Who knows, maybe Marge will inspire Sondra, though I doubt it." He quickly finished off his drink. "Do you want another?"

"No. What do you mean, 'inspire'?"

"Sondra has two interests in life. Fashion designing—though you'd never know it from the way she dresses—and reading the daily horoscope.'' He studied the olive in the bottom of his glass and popped it into his mouth after a moment. "She managed to get an A in Drawing last semester.''

"You should encourage her. You know, she really needs—''

"Please, don't tell me what she needs.'' He gripped his glass, knuckles whitening under the pressure. "Maybe I'm not an ideal parent, but I think I know what's best for her.'' He managed a taut smile and added in a surprisingly gentle voice, "But thanks for your concern. Like most men I'm probably conceited enough to think I know what's best for you, too.''

Alison felt her cheeks bloom with hot color. She pushed the half-finished margarita to one side and said, "Thanks for the drink.'' After a pause, she quietly continued, "You're quite persistent, aren't you?''

"Wouldn't it disappoint you if I wasn't?'' His voice was low and caused a shiver of excitement to throb deep within her.

"Don't hold your breath,'' she managed to reply. He *was* starting to get to her. Even though he'd hinted that he made no commitments, her curiosity had been aroused—and that wasn't all. The sooner she got this job done, the better. Abruptly she said, "I'll have something on Valentino's for you Monday morning.''

"Don't forget, I'm seeing you tomorrow night.'' He motioned for the check. "Would Marge be offended if I brought some wine?''

"If you like,'' she replied quietly. Why had Marge invited him? For that matter, why had she invited him? Was it just because of his daughter? When would she learn to stop trying to save the world and simply take care of herself? It wasn't her fault Blake McLaughlin had problems with his daughter, or probably every female on the planet for that matter. He was undoubtedly used to the glamorous type, not the Alison Sherwoods. But then just who was Alison Sherwood, anyway, and what kind of man did she really want? Not Blake, not this man whose voice alone sent sparks shooting through her. He wanted love with no strings, the kind that would break her heart if she let it.

"White wine would be nice," she said in a voice so cool it might have been chipped from ice.

Chapter Six

Ingrid, sure you don't want to come to dinner? It'll be no trouble." The pencil gripped between Alison's teeth muffled the question. She was finishing up a rough sketch of Valentino's, the fourth one she'd done, and it was almost five o'clock. She was hungry enough to eat the pencil.

"I'd give my eyeteeth to dine with Adonis, but I've got to drive Ted to Dulles." Ingrid flung a bright red scarf around her neck and dug into her pockets to produce matching gloves. She paused in the doorway and cocked a wary eyebrow in Alison's direction. "You sure you're doing this just to help his daughter?"

"Put your Cupid's bow away, Ms. Johnson, and go tend to Theodore. You know how starving sculptors get. Oh, and wish him luck on the show."

"I will. Ta!"

After she left, Alison let out a long sigh. Why couldn't she find someone as amiable as Ted Falkner? True, he evaded marriage as if it were a communicable disease, but that didn't stop Ingrid and him from loving each other with a passion most people only found in books. Don't complain, she counseled herself silently; you had Harry. Up until five years ago he'd been the center of Alison's life. She and Harry had had a smooth marriage. And Alison was a survivor. With Harry's life insurance benefits, she'd gambled on a dream of her own business. She'd gambled and won.

She gave a last look at her rendering for My Lady's Chamber. This one was good. She'd color it in pinks and deep burgundy instead of the fire-engine red and flaming flamingos. Deep velvet and satin in an updated Victorian. Leaning back in her chair, she rubbed tight neck muscles. Flicking out the light above the drafting board, she decided to call it a day. God only knew what the evening would bring, aside from her mother's Friday-night dinner special. Alison remembered with a smile how Blake had consumed five strips of tempeh bacon without batting an eye. Most men would have balked at the thought of fake meat . . . but then Blake wasn't most men.

The house was in its usual pandemonium when Alison arrived. She hadn't even gotten out of her coat before Robin flounced into the living room and shrieked, "Eric cheats at Monopoly! He took my Reading Railroad when I went to the bathroom and now he wants to sell it to me for more than I paid!" The word *paid* echoed like a pronouncement from on high.

"I did not." Eric appeared in the doorway to the family room. "You're just a silly girl, that's all."

"Am not!" She stuck her tongue out. "Granny made apple pie," Robin said in a lightning switch of mood, "to go à la mode with the ice Bean supreme." She licked her lips like a hungry alligator. "It's special for the big cheese and his kids. What is a big cheese anyway, Mom?'' Without waiting for a reply, she scrambled across the room and seized on the black Persian who'd just emerged from the porch. ''Payowakit and Ramarama don't get along. Rama says black cats are bad luck, but Granny Marge says—''

''Please, I don't think I want to hear it.'' Alison headed for the closet, hung up her coat and turned to Robin. ''Have you set the table yet?''

''It's Eric's turn,'' she sniffed, and plopped down onto the floor to begin petting the squirming cat. ''But Rama did it.''

''Is...Rama still here?'' Alison offered a fervent prayer that she'd gone back to her guru.

''Yep. She's gonna serve dinner, but she made Granny promise to tie up Dog. Sure hope he doesn't piddle again.'' Payowakit managed to get free and scooted to the kitchen. Robin scrambled after her in hot pursuit.

Was Ramarama going to become a permanent fixture? Alison was contemplating this when the doorbell rang. Pete and Eric raced past her, reaching the front door at the same time. They grappled with the knob, flung the door open and stepped back. ''C'mon in, Willy,'' Pete said. Over his shoulder he yelled, ''Hey, Mom, Willy 'n his Dad and some girl are here.''

Everyone started talking at once, Dog began to howl from his confinement, and a clatter of pans reverberated from the kitchen. Suddenly the kitchen door swung open, and Robin appeared with Payowakit secure in her arms. ''Rama says kitty will sour the dinner.''

''Put the cat in your room, Robin, and let Dog out, and—'' Alison took a deep breath and whirled back to her guests who stood by the still-open door. She rushed forward, slammed the door shut and with a fixed smile said,

"Come in and let me take your coats." Her words were garbled, and she felt incredibly uncomfortable.

Blake laughed as he shrugged out of a suede lambskin-lined jacket. He handed it to her and said, "Domestic tranquility?"

"Don't be funny. Not now." Eyeing the bottle of wine in his hands, she added, "I think I'll need a glass of that. Thanks."

"Don't mention it." Turning to his daughter, he said, "Alison, this is Sondra, Sondra, Ms. Sherwood."

"Oh, please call me Alison." The girl responded to this with a tight smile and stared absently at the floor.

At this point Marge waltzed through the door, carrying a silver tray with several tall wineglasses. An apron was carelessly draped over the sequined sleeve of her silver dress.

"Greetings! Greetings!" she sang out in dramatic tones. "Such weather we're having!" Setting the tray on the coffee table, she scurried forward, still trailing the apron but looking regal, nevertheless. "It has been such a day. I've practically had to teach Ramarama how to boil water. But, poor dear, she tries so hard."

"Dinner smells great!" Willy said, handing Alison his duffle coat.

"C'mon, we're getting ready to play Trivial Pursuit," Pete said, "but its strictly a guy's game." He puffed his chest up and Eric nodded in agreement.

Robin reappeared, Dog in tow, "You're just afraid we're smarter!" She grinned at him.

"Girls!" Pete taunted as he swaggered toward the family room.

"Humph!" Robin trounced forward, a determined look on her face. "Mommy, make them let us play. They're a bunch of meanies."

"All of you, stop this! I mean, right now." Alison paused. In a dangerously low voice she said, "If you boys can't let the girls play, then no one will play. Is that understood?"

"Aw, Mom!"

"Now, now, let's all be agreeable," Marge offered as she gestured toward the living room. "Do as your mother says or no dessert." The boys sighed in unison, and one was heard to utter, "Dumb girls!" With that, the squabbling cluster of children headed toward the family room.

"How splendid of you to bring wine, Blake! I am getting a bit low on the dandelion." She gave a fluttery sigh. "But then it's so popular, especially with Ramarama. I suppose it does help to calm her nerves."

"Rama's been at the wine? Isn't that against her code?" Blake withdrew a frosty green bottle of champagne and placed it on the dining room table.

Marge swept forward, clapping her hands in ecstasy, and murmured, "The king of wine! How superlative... You needn't worry about our Rama, we'll just give her one glass."

"Our Rama?" Alison repeated, hoping she'd heard wrong.

"Oh, heavens, didn't I tell you? Hannah called and said 'The Real You' seminar was such a success that she's decided to return to Hollywood and seek her true fortune."

"Return to Hollywood?"

"Alison, must you repeat everything like some vulgar parrot?" Marge gave an unnecessary pat to her perfectly coiffed hair. "Hannah made a monumental discovery during her past-life regression. She had been a silent-screen star who died at the height of her career. It's time for her to come into her own. Isn't it all too grand?"

"Mother, please!"

"I jest not." With a toss of her head she started for the kitchen.

"Okay, she was a silent-movie star. Which one? Or is that asking too much?"

"You mustn't press the ethers, my dear. When she's strong enough, it will be revealed. Now, if you'll excuse me, I'll just see how Rama is doing."

Blake remained silent, a shadow of a smile on his lips.

"Now, don't you start! Our Rama, replacing Hannah who's off to Hollywood to reclaim her lost fame! If Mama hadn't encouraged her in this ridiculousness, we'd still have her!" Alison threw up her arms in near despair. "You know, I just can't run this house and my business, too, not with the—"

Blake closed the gap between them and enfolded her in his arms, effectively silencing her with an infinitely gentle kiss. His arms tightened their hold, drawing her against the lean warmth of his body. Lips parted against lips, and Alison felt herself tremble and melt into the circle of his embrace as she welcomed this assault upon her senses. Their breaths mingled, hearts beating in unison. His hands, strong and powerful, slid against her mauve silk dress, electrifying her skin, and slipping lower, pressing her to him. Slowly his lips drew back, but still lingering a mere breath away.

There were no words for what he felt—for the unspoken need that ripped through him. He heard her quick intake of breath, and gazing into emerald eyes, saw the banked fires within. He felt her tremble with desire and vulnerability.

Sounds from the kitchen drew them apart, yet one of his callused palms still caressed the side of her face. His voice was low and husky. "We're about to be interrupted."

"Yes." Her voice was barely audible. "Someone might come in, and—"

He tilted her face toward him. "And think I'm a pretty lucky man." Slowly he stepped back. She was right. It might not look too good, especially if Sondra or one of the other children came in. Damn! There must be some way to get her alone. From the looks of things it was going to be a cozy evening; just the eight of them, not counting the animals, possible drop-ins and Ramarama. But then he'd known that from the start. What he didn't bargain on was the effect Alison was having on him. Didn't she have any idea about how he felt? He wanted to kiss her and to keep on kissing her, to feel every inch of her as she pulsated beneath him.

Ramarama appeared in the doorway and began clanging an Oriental gong. She had on her Buddha-like smile and did everything but bow. "Dinner! Dinner!" she called before she floated back into the kitchen.

Blake caught the startled expression on Alison's face. Could anything possibly go right? If he had anything to do with it, it would. He leaned toward Alison and whispered, "I'm claiming you for Act III."

"I . . . I don't know my lines," was her shaky reply.

"Don't worry, I'll cue you." With an inscrutable smile, he picked up the champagne, eased off the cork and filled two glasses. He noticed her fingers shook slightly as she accepted her glass. "Here's to Act III," he said lightly. Her cheeks flamed, and he thought she might say something, but all five children chose that moment to charge into the dining room. Dog began to race around the table, barking frantically.

"Pete, put Dog on the front porch. I don't think I'm up to another of Rama's spells."

"Gee, Mom, Dog likes Rama." Pete shifted from one foot to the other, "'Sides, we always let him sit at the table."

"Put him out!" Alison repeated.

"C'mon, Dog," Pete muttered sullenly as he led him to the door.

It was on the tip of Blake's tongue to ask which chair Dog occupied, but he decided there was no point in adding fuel to the fire. At least Sondra was on her good behavior, and for once, looking her age, more or less. Maybe Alison was right. Perhaps his daughter just needed contact with some decent kids. True, the Sherwood household was a bit wacky, but he had to admit it had a warmth his lacked.

"And Sondra knew every answer in the Arts and Entertainment category," Robin added triumphantly as she scooped up the final morsel of apple pie.

"Yeah, not bad for a girl. I'll give her that," Eric conceded as he held his plate for seconds.

They'd been discussing their unfinished game of Trivial Pursuit, with Robin and Sondra playing against Pete and Eric. Willy had acted as watchguard. Watchguards, they informed the grown-ups, were invented out of necessity.

Blake looked around the table at the odd assortment of people seated there. Marge, in her silver lamé gown with matching fingernail polish, had been giving a rundown of everyone's astrological sign. Ramarama, in quivering white, had consumed only one dish of apple pie. Under Marge's encouragement, she announced she'd begun a diet so she would attract her divine partner. The five children, remarkably contained, had only had one argument. And there was Alison, trying to remain unruffled and looking incredibly sexy in a mauve dress of luscious silk. Her lovely dark hair—once again in a Gibson girl—was appealingly disheveled. He longed to unpin it and run his fingers through it. There was a magic about her that made him think the wildest thoughts, even in these unlikely surroundings, which were hardly romantic.

"Rama and I will do the cleaning up," Marge announced as she pushed her chair back from the table. "Children, help clear, then you can continue your game." She eyed Alison and Blake for a moment before saying, "And you two probably need to discuss business."

"No, Mother, really, let me do the dishes!" Alison scrambled from the table. "You have on your good dress."

"My word, you make it sound as if I only have one! Besides, what are aprons for?" She winked at Blake, picked up her plate and added, "Rama, you wash, and I'll dry. I want to finish telling you my views on dairy products." Her voice trailed off as she pushed her way through the swinging door.

She knows, Blake thought. "Shall we discuss business?" he asked with a poker face as the children scooped the plates from the table.

"I believe you gave me carte blanche." Her voice was breezy, with only a hint of a tremor that betrayed the memory of a kiss. A single kiss that still tingled on her lips with a promise of so much more. For Alison, everything was happening too fast, too soon, and yet her body ached for this man whose magic touch sent quicksilver and fire through her veins.

"How about a breath of fresh air. We can even talk about carte blanche, if you like." He paused. "You'll be safe, I assure you," he said, heading for the coatrack as if he already lived there. "You, me and Dog!"

"He's part Doberman, so watch out!"

"I believe Dog is part everything, but I doubt he'll attack me. We're old friends." He slipped into his suede coat and with a flair held her red cape out like a matador. She laughed as she snatched it away, sidestepped him and headed out the door.

"Oh, look, the snow is sticking!" she said, slowly walking down the steps. Dog bounded ahead of them, barking joyously at this unexpected treat. Alison turned to face Blake, her green eyes dancing in the lamplight. Large snowflakes were sticking to her lashes and quickly settling a mantle of white on her red hood. "I love winter."

A cloud of mist escaped her mouth. There was something about her lips when she smiled at Blake that made him want to kiss her often. He wanted to remove the red cape and all the other layers of protection that she wrapped around herself. Why couldn't she see that she and he would be so good together?

"Actually, I don't love the rainy damp days and the frozen slush, but on nights like this, it's wonderful." With a twinge, he realized her words would breathe life into the coldest night. He thought of her next to him, warm and sweet in surrender, her dark hair spilling across white sheets, her skin aglow from the light of the fireplace. Then it could snow outside until hell froze over. He stepped closer to her, his breath now quickening. A tightness settled deep within him. Their eyes locked and neither looked away. His, dark with desire, reflected the jewel tones of hers.

"Alison—" He moved even closer, but she backed off, her hand connecting with an elm tree behind her.

"The snow does make it seem a bit warmer—"

He reached out and drew her toward him, repeating her name before his lips touched hers in a kiss that whispered across her lips and drew a sigh from her.

She heard the sigh and wondered where it came from; someplace inside her that had been as frozen as the limbs of the elm above them, a forgotten pain that had been turned over. She pushed against Blake's chest. "Please, no."

"You don't mean that." He spoke the words against her lips as he kissed the protest away, his arms wrapping around her, drawing her against his warmth. He could feel her body sway against his as all the will to resist him finally snapped. His own passion licked through his veins like a fire as he felt her hands slide through his hair and down to the nape of his neck. A soft moan escaped her. His kiss lingered against her mouth. On impulse his lips trailed across her cheek and down her neck. Her scent filled him with need as a misty heat rose all around them. His hands slipped beneath the cape and sought out her roundness.

"I want you, Alison," he heard himself saying thickly just before he reclaimed her mouth in a hard kiss that was hot and demanding. She wanted him just as much as he wanted her. He could feel it in the way she moved sensuously against him in the rhythm that all lovers know so well. He felt her arch into his embrace, welcoming the feel of his hands on her breasts and his tongue as it parted her lips and dove within their honeyed recesses.

Through the rising passion, she felt the now-familiar weakness flow through her and was only vaguely aware of a warning bell going off in her head. But her body responded with a will of its own, yearning for this man to carry her someplace warm, where they could feel skin on skin, and to know the length of his body against hers, to feel him deep within her. She wanted him, needed him. What was the use of denying it? All rational arguments were swept away. There would be no commitments from this man. He might walk out on her. But at this moment none of that mattered. He was whispering her name in her ear over and over; then slowly he pulled back.

"Does it take a snowstorm to warm you up, my little Eskimo?" His voice was rough with passion, but there was a thread of humor, as well. "You know it *is* a little chilly."

Alison took a steadying breath as she snuggled closer. "It was your idea to come out here and discuss business, I believe."

"You are my top priority. Number one on my agenda. And since you're determined to wrap up Valentino's in record time, I guess I'll have to move a little faster, too, to protect my interest."

Alison stiffened slightly, slowly disengaged herself and pulled her cape around her.

"Hey, Alison, what's wrong?" He touched her shoulder, but she shrugged it off.

"It is chilly out here," she replied in a quivering voice.

"That didn't seem to bother you a few minutes ago." Instinctively he brushed her cheek.

"Don't do that." She turned her face from him as confused feelings riotously surfaced and clamored for attention.

"Don't do what? This?" He cupped her face in his hands and traced the curve of her chin. "Or this?" He leaned forward, breathed softly in her ear and murmured, "Or maybe this?" His mouth descended with a restraint that echoed through his body. Working his lips over hers, he parted them until she responded with a little sound in her throat. He drew back and slowly said, "I'm not much with words of love, and there's probably some things I've done wrong in this relationship, but give me a chance."

Alison just looked at him. Her response stuck in her throat, her blood drummed in her ears, and her body trembled. But she knew reality was just around the corner. Life did not have fairy-tale endings. There was no room in her life for love. She pressed her lips together and took a step back. Drawing her arms across her chest, she knew she was raising her armor again. The frozen place in her heart must not thaw—not now.

"I can't think," she said on a frosty exhalation.

Blake let out a pent-up breath. "I'm a patient man." With a smile he added, "Up to a point."

Dog could be heard barking in the distance. Oh, Lord, Alison thought, he's probably turned over the neighbor's garbage cans again. She could handle that, she could handle her children, she could probably even handle Rama-whatever-her-name-was. But Blake McLaughlin? No, not yet.

Once inside, the lingering aroma of apple pie greeted them. The house was filled with happy sounds: children laughing in the family room, Rama and Marge actually singing in the kitchen, and someone had started a blazing fire on the hearth. Her home was a warm and happy haven, but Alison felt chilled to her heart.

Chapter Seven

What a lovely day you'll have, Alison, dear. Though I hope you won't get bored." Marge took a slow, thoughtful bite of what looked like scrambled eggs, then turning her attention to Rama, said, "This should be a landmark weekend for you. I'm so glad you agreed to go."

Rama, eyes cast down, merely nodded and indulged in another nibble of dried toast. Alison was beginning to think the woman had taken a vow of silence.

"This tofu needs a little something extra," Marge suddenly said.

"Eggs?" Alison suggested wearily. She hadn't slept well, and the fact that the coffee jar was empty didn't help her mood.

"Don't speak heresy," Marge scolded mildly. "Think of those poor chickens, all cooped up." She drew in a long breath before adding, "But I can see something's bothering you which, if I'm not mistaken, has to do with your Mr. McLaughlin."

"He's not *my* Mr. McLaughlin, and he never was."
With a sigh she finished off her juice, picked up her plate
and headed for the sink. Their cheery breakfast nook was
comprised of a large oak table and ladder-back chairs that
fit snugly into a corner of the kitchen. Sunlight streamed
in through windows that faced a yard in need of mowing.
Alison scraped her plate and put it into the dishwasher.
"And nothing's bothering me."

"I know better than to argue with you. However, that
Mars-Saturn aspect is enough to make anyone irritable.
Look at the way you acted toward Blake last night."

"And just how did I act?"

"At the end of the evening you were quite distant, considering all things. But then you'll have the weekend to re-
charge."

"I'll probably go in to work. I want to get this Valentino project finished as soon as possible." The sound of a
banging door was followed by Robin's wail as she ran into
the kitchen.

"Eric took my bubble gum!"

"Did not! You owe it to me 'cause you and Sondra lost
Trivial Pursuit. 'Member?" Eric circled around to the
kitchen table and helped himself to a sticky bun.

"Liar! Liar!" Robin grabbed a bun in defense and
pushed it into her mouth with a vengeance.

"Didn't you all have enough for breakfast?" Alison
asked in exasperation.

"Make him give me back my bubble gum!" Robin
stomped her foot. "Me and Sondra—"

"Sondra and I," Marge quickly corrected as she retrieved the sticky buns. "You'll get quite sick if you eat any
more of these."

"Sondra and I did not bet my gum to that...creep." She licked her fingers and stuck her tongue out at him. "You're just mad 'cause we get to go on the day trip, too."

"Am not."

Alison looked up from the half-loaded dishwasher. "I thought Sondra was in the junior high."

"They get to go, too." Robin's gaze swept the table in search of more food.

"It's a silly trip," Eric mumbled, popping the rest of the bun in his mouth. "Who wants to go to cruddy old Williamsburg and look at a bunch of people in cruddy clothes!"

"Don't you know any other word except 'cruddy'?" Alison asked as she started up the dishwasher.

"Yeah, I bet they don't even have a—McDonald's—anywhere near that cruddy place."

"Eric! You know what I've told you about these fast-food places." Marge straightened visibly and looked at her watch. "Oh, heavens, Rama and I must be going. Now Alison, if you should need us for anything, we can be reached at the Bonnie Blue Motel on Route 1. You know, it's the same astrology convention I go to every year. We'll be back late Sunday night." She clapped her hands in near ecstasy. "Imagine, I'm bringing a Triple Pisces with a T square in earth. It simply boggles the mind. I declare it does." Pulling out her compact, she pressed the edges of her false eyelashes, powdered her nose and snapped the compact shut. She wore a suit in a shocking shade of fuchsia with a frilly silk blouse. It reminded Alison of the pink flamingos.

"Are Triple Pisces rare?" Rama asked in a hushed and unexpected voice. She blinked dark eyes that resembled raisins tossed in a bowl of cream of wheat. Everyone turned to her as if she'd just performed some miracle.

"Rare as hen's teeth," Marge assured her. "You'll be a cause célèbre."

Alison gave her mother a peck on the cheek. "Have a good time."

"We shall, we shall. Come Rama!" Leaning down, she kissed Robin and pressed something in her hand. "That's what we used to call 'mad money,' but if you must buy gum, make sure it's sugarless."

Pete and Eric suddenly appeared, both looking bedraggled, and said, "Hey, how 'bout us?" A large pink bubble exploded from Eric's mouth.

"When you stop acting like hooligans and start treating your sister nicely, then I shall consider it."

No sooner had Marge and Rama left, than a black-and-yellow school bus beeped its horn and all three children ran screaming out the front door.

"Obey your teachers," Alison called after them and waved until the bus was out of sight. With a sigh she headed back for a morning of cleaning house. A howl from the basement made her realize Dog was still locked away. Oh, God, not another puddle! Rama would have to get along with the animals, or she'd have to go! Triple Pisces notwithstanding.

It was well past noon when she finally finished straightening the house. It was amazing how housecleaning could help clear away the mental cobwebs, or at least diminish them. Still, Blake McLaughlin's entry into her life had stirred up feelings and needs Alison wasn't sure she was ready to face. Yes, needs; she needed Blake like a flower needs sun and water. Yet she chose to hide behind her mask of self-sufficiency, family and career. The painful realization that both Ingrid and her mother were right didn't help things. Besides, what did she have to offer

Blake? The truth was he was a high-powered businessman who moved in the fast lane and dealt in megabucks. Although Alison had a successful career, she could hardly match his luminary status.

Enough! she said to herself, giving the mop a final shake out the back door. Things could certainly be worse. At least her cousin had picked up Studs and Playboy. Now all she had to contend with was finding homes for Payowakit's brood. The mother cat knew something was afoot, for she had hidden her young in the back of Marge's closet. Yes, on the domestic end, Alison had things under control. She'd shower, grab a bite to eat and spend the afternoon working on Valentino's.

Alison was just drying off from a shower when the doorbell rang. Throwing on a terry cloth robe, she ran to the door.

"Blake!" She backed up, holding the robe together.

"May I come in?" He held a gold candy box and a single rose in one hand and a bottle of champagne in the other. "Godiva chocolates. Five pounds, remember?"

"Five pounds of Godiva chocolates? Do you want me to turn into the Goodyear Blimp?"

"I don't care what you look like, so long as you let me come in." He offered a twisted smile. "Besides, I won't let you eat all of it. I do have to protect my interests."

Standing there with the sunlight slanting across his rugged features, Alison felt her pulses leap traitorously. What was it about him that caused her to run hot and cold?

"Yes, do come in," she heard herself answer softly, wondering if he could hear the tremor in her voice. He was dressed casually. An open sheepskin coat revealed an Irish fisherman's sweater and snug-fitting jeans that looked incredibly sexy. But it was the hand-tooled cowboy boots that stopped her in her tracks. Her gaze flew back to meet his.

"I don't live in a three-piece suit," he commented mildly as he pushed the door shut. "There *are* other sides to me."

"I imagined there were," Alison replied as she backed farther into the living room and grappled for something more to say. "It's a little early for dandelion wine, but you're welcome to join me for lunch."

"Sounds great." He thrust the chocolates and champagne at her. "We can have the champagne later, but you'd better hide Godiva from Marge. I'm afraid she wouldn't approve. They're made with sugar."

"Don't worry," she assured him, placing the chocolates and champagne on the coffee table. "Marge and Rama have gone to an astrological conference and won't be back till Sunday night."

"Then you're here—" he paused significantly before adding "—alone?"

"Not quite," she called over her shoulder as she headed up the stairs. "There's my ferocious dog, the cat and several kittens."

"I stand forewarned."

She smiled down at him. "Good. Give me ten minutes to dress, then we can eat. There's a Chinese place that delivers. Why don't you give them a call? The telephone number's on the side of the phone in the kitchen." She vanished into the upstairs hall.

"What do you want?" He was standing in the middle of the living room, holding the red rose and feeling more alive than he could ever remember.

"Their sweet-and-sour vegetarian special, a bucket of rice and two fortune cookies," she called back.

Picking up the champagne, he started for the kitchen but paused before the Edgar Allan Poe whatnot that held various knickknacks and photos. One was of Alison in her wedding dress. It was a simple white sheath, and instead of a veil she wore a broad-rimmed white hat. A companion photo was obviously the groom. He had blond hair, wore glasses and had a casual, friendly air about him. Other photos included the usual adorable baby shots. There was only one other of Alison and her husband, on a sunny stretch of beach, and they were both laughing and squinting into the camera. Feeling like a snoop, Blake headed for the kitchen and ordered their lunch from Chang's Chinese Carryout. He put the champagne in the refrigerator, plopped the thirsty rose into a glass of water and went back to the living room.

Restlessly he paced the room, trying to gather his thoughts. He'd never met a woman like Alison before, nor had he wanted a woman as much as he wanted her. He was all too aware that he wasn't ready to make a reckless declaration of love, yet he knew he had to have her in his life. There was something so very soothing about her presence, though Lord knows the cyclone of madcap activity that usually surrounded her was hardly conducive to the intimacy Blake needed. Still, he admired the way she coped with it all and even managed to raise three decent kids. He paused once again in front of the wedding photo and realized how much they had in common. They'd both lost their loved ones.

The doorbell interrupted his thoughts. The restaurant definitely lived up to its motto, Chang's Speedy Delivery.

By the time Alison got downstairs, he had set the table and put the steaming food into bowls. The lone rose, placed in a jelly glass, stood as centerpiece.

"How elegant," Alison exclaimed as she entered the dining room.

"And your presence completes the picture," Blake murmured approvingly as his gaze roved across her. She was wearing a plum-colored silk blouse and gray slacks that hugged her in a way that made Blake want to scoop her up in his arms and make passionate love in front of the fireplace. To hell with chow mein!

"Smells divine, doesn't it?" Alison said, effectively dampening his amorous fantasy. Sitting at the table, she began spooning out aromatic sweet-and-sour vegetables over mounds of fluffy rice. Throughout the meal, Alison managed to keep the conversation light and impersonal. She was not up to dealing with the glint in Blake's eye. He, however, was not one to be put off indefinitely.

"About last night," Blake began as he casually broke his fortune cookie in half, "I really meant what I said about being a patient man, and I want you to know you mean more to me than..." He let the thought trail off, but his eyes narrowed and glittered with dark fires. Reaching across the table, he interlaced his fingers with hers.

A tingle of excitement ran up her arm as he slowly drew her hand to his lips and kissed the palm. It was an infinitely gentle gesture that made Alison deliciously aware of the liquid fire within her. She swallowed and tried to look away from his penetrating gaze for she knew her feelings were plain to see.

He released her hand. "I thought we might take in a couple of museums on the mall, then after I've worn you out sufficiently, we could stop off for dinner somewhere, *and* be back before the kids return from their outing. Too bad it's not an overnight trip." He gave Alison a wicked wink and added, "I'm only human." The look in his eyes, as they caressed her face, emphasized this fact.

"I had planned on working on Valentino's today," she said, attempting to quiet her racing heart. "I'd hate to get behind in my work."

"I suppose I'd have no choice but to sack you," he murmured, obviously pleased with his pun. "But in the meantime, why don't you throw caution to the winds and enjoy the day off. I've got my best behavior on, or can't you tell?" He rose.

"Mr. McLaughlin, I think you're conceited!" Alison laughed in spite of herself as she began to clear the table.

After three hours of gallery gazing, as Blake called it, they decided to try a new Japanese restaurant in Georgetown.

"I understand they have a lot of vegetarian dishes," he assured her as they followed a kimono-clad hostess to a low-lying corner table. Colorful cotton cushions surrounded it, and a small lantern spilled light on the black-lacquered wood.

"Hope you don't mind sitting on the floor," Blake teased as they removed their shoes before situating themselves on the cushions.

"At this point I'd sit anywhere. Oh, my aching feet. Next time we go gallery hopping, remind me to wear my sneakers!"

"Hey, whose idea was it to hit every museum on the mall?"

"Guilty as charged, though it was fun. And as for sitting Seiza, that's what they call it when you sit on your heels, I rather like it." She let out a long sigh. "Feels good!"

"You sound like a seasoned pro when it comes to things Japanese."

"Mother's responsible for that. She went through an Oriental phase when she would only eat brown rice with chopsticks. That was right before she became enamored with past-life regressions."

Pausing to look around, she noted, "This is quite a nice restaurant." It had clean, uncluttered lines, lending an air of tranquility. Diffused light shone through translucent white screens, and tatami straw mats covered the floor. A quiet Japanese melody could be heard, and the pungent aroma of ginger filled the air. There were several other couples near them, and a large party seemed to be enjoying itself at the end of the room.

"Would you like some sake before we order?" Blake asked. When Alison nodded, the waitress bowed twice and left. After a pause, Blake unexpectedly asked, "You don't really believe in that business about past life, do you? I can see some validity to astrology, but the rest of it—"

"Oh, I'd rather like to think I was a countess, or perhaps a kadin living in a harem. Something exotic and mysterious." Alison suddenly felt relaxed and happy in Blake's company. Today had been a gift for her. They had actually had fun together!

The meal surpassed anything Alison had eaten in a long time. The sake went right to her head, leaving her slightly giddy. They had a second carafe during the main course, which consisted of a soothing clear broth and some delicious raw fish called sashimi, which was accompanied by a hot horseradish. A cucumber salad and delicate swirls of sea vegetable over sautéed rice completed their meal.

"What, no fortune cookie?" Blake asked, surveying the dessert menu.

"That's Chinese," Alison answered on a laugh. "By the way, what did your cookie say this afternoon?" She feigned a casual interest as she continued perusing the dessert menu.

"It assured me of success in everything if I remained true to myself. You know how inscrutable those fortunes can be. How about yours?"

"I'm going to be taking a cruise in a sunny climate. It didn't have any qualifiers, so I suppose I can be as rotten as I like and still hit the jackpot." She smiled over the menu. "I'll have the Orange Boat for dessert, in preparation for my journey. Then, if you like, we can stop at the store and get a box of fortune cookies and just eat away until we find one that suits us while we wait for the children." Her smile faded slowly. The gleam in Blake's eyes told her fortune cookies were the last thing on his mind. He'd stated quite clearly what he wanted: her. And he was a man who usually got what he wanted. Alison felt a little shiver race up her spine at the thought of an uninterrupted, well, almost uninterrupted evening with him. The plain fact was that his presence alone, not to mention his touch or the way he kissed, made her feel like a weak-kneed teenager. Try as she might, there was no way to hide from this man, and she was beginning to wonder if she wanted to anyway.

As the silence lengthened, she plunged her fork into the Orange Boat dessert and added as casually as she could, "The kids will be getting back around eight-thirty."

"That will give us enough time alone," Blake replied as he poured more tea, "though I might eventually kidnap you to that Caribbean island your fortune cookie promised."

"Oh, you might?" she teased back, hoping the tremor in her voice wasn't that detectable.

"I might."

It had started snowing while they were in the restaurant. Since they'd left the car at her house, they started walking the six blocks up Thirty-first Street to her house on Tulip Lane. The wind had picked up, and snow seemed to be swirling out of Alaska with an intensity reminiscent of the storm of '66.

"It's so cold," Alison chattered as she attempted to burrow deeper into her wool cape. Blake's arm encircled her shoulders and afforded some additional warmth.

"You know, we could have called for a taxi," he said above the keening wind.

"Oh, but this is so much more fun!" she called back. "Think how nice it will be to start a fire, eat chocolates and sip champagne." She was feeling reckless and a little giddy. It had been such a perfect day. She glanced up at him and in the glow from the streetlight was once again stuck by the dark planes of his rugged face, such a contrast to the dazzling whiteness that surrounded them. Looking down at her, his jet eyes seemed to crackle, and she felt drawn into their depths.

By the time they crested Thirty-first Street Alison felt winded, but Blake looked as if he did this sort of thing several times a day. "One more block," she said through numb lips.

"Are you ready for that Caribbean cruise?" he teased as they turned down Tulip Lane.

"Tomorrow isn't soon enough!"

"Don't tell me my little Eskimo is about to freeze?" He drew her closer until she could practically hear his heartbeat.

Far from freezing, she was melting right into his arms.

Dog greeted them at the front door. Alison knew there was undoubtedly a puddle somewhere in the house, but she would tend to that later. Dog seemed quite content to race around the snowy backyard. Payowakit languished across the back of the velvet wing chair and merely blinked her topaz eyes in their direction.

Alison stood for a moment in the middle of the living room, her snowy cap shedding melting snow on Marge's Oriental rug. "The place feels empty," she remarked. "As if there's been a party and all the guests have gone home." She allowed Blake to help her out of the cape.

"I should think you'd enjoy a little peace and quiet." He hung their coats on an antique clothes stand located by the door. Then, crossing to the fireplace, he hunkered down and began shredding newspaper and stacking kindling. "I'll have this blazing in no time. Why don't you get the champagne and let's celebrate."

"Celebrate?" She was doing it again. Marge called it "polly parroting," and it was Alison's worst habit.

"Celebrate," Blake confirmed with a twinkle in his eye. As if it were understood, he added, "The future."

"Oh. Sure." Alison's heart did a curious dance. "The champagne you brought . . . I'll get it."

By the time she returned, the hearth was blazing with accompanying popping and crackling sounds. Blake was reclining before the flames, making a study of them. Wordlessly he turned toward Alison. She felt a flush creep onto her cheeks. Slowly she knelt beside him, placing the tray with champagne, glasses and a plate of crackers to one side. Without saying a thing, he stretched over and picked up the bottle. Aiming it away from them, he eased the cork from the bottle and sent it flying across the room. They both burst out laughing and scrambled for a glass to catch the overflow.

"You did that like a pro," Alison said, clutching the long-stemmed glass. As he poured champagne, her gaze trailed all six feet two of him. He was long, lean and with enough magnetism for three men. His unself-conscious charisma made him all the more appealing. He didn't *have* to try to do anything. He looked great in whatever he wore. This evening's cable-knit sweater had been tossed to one side, and the blue-and-white oxford shirt that was unfastened at the neck allowed a glimpse of black curly hair. It was just enough to make her want to touch that broad expanse of chest. She knew he was strong, for she had felt the breadth of him last night, and the memory had tattooed itself on the soft curve of her hips and breast. The thought of this intimacy sent a warm feeling through her.

He proposed a toast to her eyelashes, and they both laughed and clinked glasses. Her inner warmth increased as she raised her glass and hailed his dark eyes. In the glow from the fireplace those eyes sparkled, and in the silence that fell he reached out and traced the line of her face.

"You know, you have the craziest effect on me, my little Eskimo." He came closer still, blocking the flames from her view. She blinked as a tremor of longing shot through her. Closing her eyes, she felt herself being pulled into his embrace. She'd never been dizzy in her life, but she was now. Breathing deeply, she took in wood smoke, his spicy cologne and the very essence of him. The clock struck eight. Soon the children would come barreling through the door. The thought was pushed to one side as his lips nibbled the corner of her mouth and his breathing came faster. One hand held her close and the other slipped down the front of her blouse, rasping across the silk that lay between his palms and her flesh.

Alison ached with the need for that touch. All of her fears were now sleeping. She *needed* Blake as surely as he needed her. There was no use denying it. Had it really been five lonely years since she'd been with a man? Now all the passion and yearning welled up inside her, demanding satisfaction. Somehow she sensed she could trust him, and even though their future was still on shaky ground, she knew that they were destined to be lovers. She heard his voice whisper her name, then his breath was warm in her ear.

"Alison, Alison, how I want you. You've driven me crazy since that first time I saw you." His lips sent a flurry of kisses down her neck as he drew her closer to him. There had never been a woman quite like Alison, but he didn't know how to tell her that. For that matter, he wasn't sure exactly what his feelings were. But this need, this desire knifed through him as his mouth searched out that sweetness her lips offered, tasting and wanting more.

"Blake..." Her voice was muffled against the hungry pressure. Slowly her hands curled around his neck and, creeping higher, lost themselves in his hair. The ticktock of the grandfather clock and the crackle of the fire receded into the background. She heard no sound but that of their mingled breaths and heartbeats. There was no feeling but that of the lean, questing body pressed against her softness. A sweet, wanton hunger sprang up between them, and she heard herself murmur, "I want you, too." Moaning at the penetrating expertise of his tongue as it sought out her mouth, she felt herself surrender completely to him. The long lines of her body molded to his, caught up in timeless interplay.

Blake pulled back and sought the glimmer in her eyes that matched the passion in his. His voice was ragged, and she knew he was exerting every ounce of his self-control. "Our timing *is* a little off," he said softly, cupping her face in his hands. He added with a hint of humor, "What we need is that island paradise your fortune cookie foretold. Right now!"

"It would be nice," she murmured in agreement. Her hands were splayed across his chest, feeling the heat beneath his touch, longing for him.

Blake's gaze rested on the single button he'd undone. Gently his fingers started to fasten it, but lingered at the opening. Slipping down to the next button, he undid it and, pulling back the plum-colored silk blouse, brushed against the fullness of her breast. A growl sounded deep in his throat as his hand eased beneath her lacy bra. Alison pulled him toward her with an urgency that surprised him. Intense pleasure shot through him as his desire mounted and hardened. His lips followed the path his hand had blazed. He could hear her heart and her breathing. He could feel the need and passion fill every inch of her as he continued tormenting and caressing her. *And I need her.* Again the thought burst upon him, tightening the coil within, but when her hands—trembling with the same need—drew him even closer, he felt the hunger as one starved at a banquet.

The clock struck the half hour. Blake took a shuddering breath, and, raising his head, looked at Alison and all her loveliness, touched now with a rich passion. Her lips were parted, her emerald eyes half-closed and filled with longing, and her dark thick hair was undone and spilled about her shoulders. Then there was the scent of her, sweet and sensual, that intoxicated him. As one drugged, he wanted more and more.

Dog let out a howl as he thundered into the room, then plopped at the front door to continue his plaintive barking. Blake fumbled madly with the little pearl buttons of Alison's blouse, but she stayed his hand.

"Let me do it." She was smiling softly, but the glimmer was still in her green eyes. He hoped it would never leave. A man could lose himself in those eyes, he thought, amazed at the transformation in this woman. Her defenses were stripped, the icy facade a meltdown, and the woman beneath as fiery and passionate as Blake had ever known. She was open to his every caress, her lips reddened with arousal, her eyes flashing with a promise of more. She was a treasure and he a pauper bereft of words.

"I guess it wasn't the children, after all," Alison said as she fastened the last button. "But it *is* better this way." She looked at him shyly, their intimacies lingering in the very air, unspoken. She knew that she would never be free of the memory of his touch. Nothing would ever be the same after this evening. Nothing.

Seeking refuge in trivialities, she steered the subject onto safer ground. "Where did you get your accent? The one that slips out every now and then?"

"Is it that bad?"

"Oh, no. I think it sounds—" she paused, then added softly "—sexy."

"You bring out the best in me." He leaned over and nuzzled her neck with playful kisses, loving the way her skin smelled, loving everything about her. "Like velvet," he murmured, his hands skimming across her cheek. "Down San Marcos way, they'd call you a pretty spectacular gal."

"Thanks." She sounded a little breathless, and he noticed those green eyes sparkling up at him—dazzling him. He'd do anything for her. "Where's San Marcos?" she asked.

"In Texas, li'l thang. Right near San Antone."

"Do you go back to visit?"

"You're getting close to the quick, but I don't suppose it will hurt to bare my soul to you. Though you have to swear on your honor not to sell my life story to a magazine." He was joking, but in a way he meant it. Suddenly

Blake wanted to share some of that shadowed past. No one really knew about the pain of growing up dirt-poor in a small Texas town.

"I promise not to capitalize on your past," Alison answered softly, "but if you want to talk about it, I'm here." Her voice sounded infinitely gentle and caring to him. Something he'd never expected to find in any woman again.

"You *are* special, Alison." He stretched out, his arms crossed behind his head, and stared thoughtfully at the dancing flames in the fireplace. "I was an only child. I don't think my dad wanted any children, and my mother died shortly after I was born. It was really my grandparents who took care of me, or tried to." Blake paused and took a deep breath. "When I was thirteen they died within six months of each other, and Dad had long since disappeared. So the courts put me in a foster home, but I became a runaway."

"You were so young."

"A little older than Sondra," he commented sadly.

"How did you live?"

"The great American dream. I hopped freight cars, rode the Mississippi, camped out with bums of every color imaginable, and hung out with the best flimflam men on the West Coast. Learned how to play cards and hold my liquor." He rolled onto his side and looked intently at her. "But from the start I knew I'd never be one of them. I didn't want to end up on the receiving end of state charity or the Salvation Army soup lines. So, when I was twenty-two, I tried on respectability and a three-piece suit. The fit was tight at first, but I got used to it." Blake paused, and on a laugh added, "Still had that rebel streak as wide as Texas in me. Proud, too. But after I invented a little gizmo, I had enough capital to invest in some real estate that took off, and so did I. I left Lenlectrics Computers and started my own business."

"Camelot," Alison supplied.

"Camelot."

"Just like that?"

He saw the wonder in her eyes and loved her for it. "Just like that, Eskimo." He stretched his long legs before him and continued his study of the hearth. "I suppose I made a lot of wise investments, and a few foolish ones." His gaze returned to Alison. She was so beautiful in the fire glow. Her cheeks were rosy and her lips so very kissable. He wanted to kiss every inch of her, slowly, savoring her sweetness.

All thoughts of kisses and the like fled from his mind as Dog let out a series of joyous yelps and began leaping at the door.

"Oh, Lord!" No sooner had Alison reached for the lamp and flicked it on than the front door burst open and five, *not* three, children scrambled in, excited and chattering and seemingly oblivious to the presence of two startled adults who were quickly composing themselves.

Sheepishly Blake said, "I told my kids to come by here after the school trip."

"Oh." Alison's eyebrows raised a trifle at this disclosure. "You were pretty sure of yourself, weren't you?"

"Guilty as charged." The look in his eye suggested he was quite sure of himself. Softly he added, "Next time the kids will have an overnight trip!"

Chapter Eight

As exasperating as the children's arrival had been, Alison knew they were the last vestige of armor keeping her from tumbling straight into Blake McLaughlin's bed. The frozen place within her was rapidly melting, and her need for him was growing with each passing day. His presence dispelled her fears, even though she was sure his idea of commitment was miles away from hers.

Even so, during the next two weeks she allowed herself that false sense of security as they worked together and took extended lunch hours. She never realized just how many art galleries there were in Washington, or how sore one's feet could become in their pursuit. The Valentino project was coming to a close, but Blake promised Alison another account and even more money.

On the home front things seemed to be going along quite well, also. Rama, having experienced a transformation during her astrological weekend, had dropped her white sheet and about ten pounds. Her guru had been charged

with embezzling funds and was put in prison. It turned out
he was a fraud from Hyattsville, Maryland, and not from
the high Himalayas. Ramarama became plain Sally Jean
Coleman from New Braunfels, Texas. Under Marge's tu-
telage, she began spouting platitudes around the house as
she ran the vacuum cleaner. She had written several affir-
mations and plastered them to the refrigerator: "I am now
attracting my perfect mate," "The universe loves me" and
"I am a winner!" Alison had to admit the change was im-
pressive. Sally Jean even went so far as to accept Payowakit and Dog.

Even Alison's children appeared to be on fairly good
behavior. Robin had fastened onto Sondra as an older and
wiser sister, and the teenage girl seemed to blossom under
this attention. Willy became an honorary member of the
Sherwood Gang and frequently spent the night. Everything seemed perfect, perhaps too perfect. But if it was a
dream, Alison didn't want to awaken. From the beginning she knew commitment and words of love wouldn't
come easily to Blake McLaughlin's lips. The fact that he
opened up at all she considered a favorable sign. She asked
no more of him, and for the time being she chose to ignore her inner voice that posed so many questions.

Still she continued to wrap herself in a rosy haze. To
celebrate the near completion of Valentino's Pleasure,
Alison decided to have a small cocktail party with a few of
her co-workers and several couples she'd met through
Blake. She was particularly fond of Lew Mathieson, who
called a spade a spade, but underneath was a romantic
through and through.

Ingrid and Ted were the first to arrive. They brought a
tray of canapés and a bottle of champagne, and, while Ted
joined the kids in the family room for some Trivial Pursuit, Ingrid insisted on fussing over the hors d'oeuvres.

"Relax, Ingrid," Alison said with a laugh as she placed the tray on the table. "And thanks for these lovely sandwiches. I don't know where you get the patience to roll them up!"

"I'm a frustrated caterer at heart," the blonde replied, patting the waistline of her creamy wool-knit dress. "You know how I am around food. Oh, well, Ted likes me this way." She picked up a tiny cucumber sandwich and popped it into her mouth. "They have my stamp of approval, as does Blake, by the way." She fingered a second canapé. "He really is a prize. But then I told you he was."

"Yes, you did," Alison agreed softly. One thing she could always count on with Ingrid was complete honesty. Much to Alison's delight, her friend and Blake had hit it off right away.

"And speaking of stamps of approval, you look fantastic. Neiman's, right?"

Alison nodded. "I couldn't resist it." She was about to add something when the phone rang. "I'll take it in the kitchen. Do you mind playing hostess?"

"Not at all." Gingerly Ingrid scooped up a handful of peanuts. "Anything to keep me away from the marvelous food!"

Sally Jean appeared in the kitchen doorway holding a platter of yet more sandwiches. "Telephone for you, Mrs. Sherwood." It still seemed strange to hear Sally Jean's voice; and stranger to be called "Mrs. Sherwood."

Marge whirled around, a carving knife in hand. "You look absolutely spectacular, my dear. I believe Sally Jean said it was Blake on the phone. Do tell him to get over here! Oh, and tell him to bring Willy's pj's; he's spending the night."

"I suppose you heard all that," Alison said, her voice light and carefree as she took the receiver.

There was a slight pause before Blake spoke. "Alison, I'm sorry, but something's come up." She heard him take a deep breath and everything froze inside her. Slowly he said, "Sondra's disappeared."

"Oh, no!" Alison drew in a breath. "Blake, you're sure she didn't leave a note you missed?"

"Positive. The police are on their way over now. They seem to think it's a runaway situation. Asked me all kinds of questions. Did I get along with my daughter? Was I happily married? Did my daughter have a boyfriend—"

"Blake," she interrupted, "I'm coming over!"

"No. Stay there until your guests leave. I'll call if anything turns up."

"Well, all right," Alison said reluctantly. "No point in alarming the others. I'll be right over as soon as everyone goes home." She hung up and quietly told her mother and Ingrid what had happened.

As soon as the last guest left, she hurriedly changed into jeans and a pullover and headed for Blake's house. Not until then did she realize how much she loved Blake, wanted to be part of his life, to bring him joy and cheer. Yet, did *he* want and need her? Even now in this crisis he was stalwart in his desire to go it alone. What did she really have to offer Blake? A feeling of deep inadequacy assailed her, ripping aside the gossamer dream of hoped-for love.

"But he does need me, or he wouldn't have called," she murmured aloud as she pulled into his driveway. She'd seen and been duly impressed by his Georgetown mansion just last week when he'd had her over for lunch. It was spacious and had high ceilings and sleek lines. It was filled with chrome and glass and wall-to-wall carpeting that was cold and lacked the personal touch. Alison suspected he'd had it redecorated after Ginny's death.

Pushing all her thoughts to one side, Alison climbed the marble steps and pressed the bell. Chimes could be heard above the faint whistling of wind. When the door opened, she fell into Blake's arms and held him as tightly as she could. Words were futile. The police had been there a while, and it seemed no stone had been left unturned.

"This is the only picture you have of her?" the investigator asked as he looked at an eight-by-ten color photo of Sondra in her grade school graduation dress.

"There are others," Blake replied wearily. "I'll get them."

He left the room, returning moments later with a photo album. Placing it on the dining room table, he flipped toward the back. "This is the most recent one." He pulled the photo from its plastic cover and handed it to the officer.

"We'll get it back to you first thing in the morning." He slid the photo into his briefcase and headed for the door.

"Officer, I have one last question." Blake ran an unsteady hand through his dark hair. "What exactly makes you think this is a runaway?"

The inspector narrowed his eyes and slowly said, "Most of these disappearances are, and there is no indication of foul play. We'll of course check everything out, but chances are good you'll hear from her before we find anything. It's hard to accept right now, but these kids almost always turn up okay."

After the police left, Blake poured two Scotches over ice, handed one to Alison and collapsed on the couch beside her. "Why?" he asked in a voice drained of all emotion. "Was I that bad a father?"

"Oh, Blake, this is no time for you to blame yourself." She reached for his hand and squeezed it gently.

"But I do." He slumped down in the couch. Resting his head back, he continued, "Yesterday morning Sondra and I had a bad fight. It was over that damn business of the boarding school."

"But I thought you'd decided to let her finish out the year before making any decisions."

"I had, but then I got to thinking about that junior high school. I just don't want her going there!" He sat forward suddenly, gripping his drink. "The point is, Sondra left the house in tears. I feel like a heel. She didn't come home until nine last night. I should have said something to her, and now she's either been abducted or run off with God knows who." He rose abruptly and began to pace. "I suppose I haven't been much of a father, and since Ginny died, this place hasn't been much of a home." He made a sweeping gesture with his glass. He was right, of course. There was nothing warm about the chrome-and-glass decor, and the sleek modular couches looked as though they belonged in the lobby of Camelot Enterprises.

Alison sipped her drink and kept these thoughts to herself. After a moment she said, "It's probably a good thing Willy's spending the night. I didn't say anything about Sondra, and I told Marge and Ingrid not to tell him anything until we know more."

"Thanks. You think of everything." He offered a smile that didn't quite reach his eyes. "Damn! I wish there were something I could do! This waiting is going to drive me crazy." He downed his drink and headed toward the bar. "If Sondra had a boyfriend, wouldn't I have known?"

"Maybe not." Alison rose and joined him. She put her drink on the bar, reached up and began to massage his neck. "I'm not saying that to upset you, but, Blake, she could have met some guy in the mall or at school. You know how kids hang out these days."

"I'm probably hiding my head in the sand." He rolled his head from side to side, enjoying the pressure of her hands.

"No more than any other parent would." She gently led him back to the couch. "I'll call home and tell them not to wait up for me. I'll stay tonight."

"Thanks," he said, smiling gratefully.

Neither of them slept that night, and after several cups of coffee, they thrashed out all the possibilities until the light of dawn. Alison fixed some toast and more coffee for Blake and made a quick trip back home to check on her children. After assuring Marge she'd get in touch with her as soon as they learned something, she hurried back to Blake. If anything, he was more distraught than ever. His usual patina, be it Brooks Brothers or rugged cowboy, was gone. He had changed into a pair of rumpled khaki pants, scuffed loafers and a shirt that looked faded and old. He had shaved, but his face was haggard and his eyes bloodshot. He greeted her at the door with a cup of coffee and led the way to the kitchen.

"Thanks for taking care of Willy. Did you tell him about Sondra?"

"No, but I did tell him that you and Sondra had had a bad fight and that she'd run off to a friend's house." Alison joined Blake at the glass-top kitchen table. The toast she'd made earlier lay untouched. "But I reassured him she'd be back this afternoon. I honestly didn't know what else to say."

"You handled it better than I would have." He poured himself more coffee. "I haven't been an ideal father. No, let me finish. I've done what I thought best, but obviously it wasn't enough. The police are right, Sondra probably has run away." He slanted Alison a painful look. "But she wouldn't have done it in the first place if I'd been there for her, any more than she'd have been hanging out in the Harbor Bar." He fingered a piece of toast thoughtfully and with a sigh slid the plate from him. "You were right about her all along."

"That's because I'm an outsider."

"Just the same, thanks." A ghost of a smile touched his lips. "That's one of the many things I like about you. When all this is straightened out, I'll be more specific, but right now I'm afraid this waiting to hear from her or the police is beginning to get to me." Impatience stamped across his face as he abruptly reached for the phone and punched the buttons. Alison listened intently as he rattled out his questions. There was a long pause before he carefully replaced the receiver.

"Damn," he muttered, his features frozen in disdain. "They have an APB out on her with hopes something will turn up in forty-eight hours. Forty-eight hours!" he snorted. He rose to his feet. "You said the teenagers hang out at the malls. So let's start combing them, everyplace you can think of!"

By the end of the day, they'd covered more malls than Alison ever imagined, finally stopping for a bite to eat at Canal Park, a fashionable glassed-in shopping arena that resembled a cross between an arboretum and a rococo greenhouse. Glass elevators whisked them from floor to floor as they scoured all three levels. Normally Alison loved shopping at this particular mall; it had an airy quality about it that the others lacked. It also offered a wide range of items from a life-size stuffed camel going for three thousand dollars to tiny doll furniture for a more reasonable sum.

"Well, we've been through Sondra's favorite malls," Alison remarked as she finished off the last of her vegetarian burrito. "She even brought Robin here."

"God knows the place is crawling with kids," Blake said as he raked his hand through his dark hair. "What on earth do they see in these places?"

"It's considered to be 'in.'" Alison took a sip of her tea before adding, "But honestly, Blake, I don't think we're going to find her in *any* mall."

"I know." Blake threw his napkin on the table in despair. "I just need to feel like I'm doing something. Can you understand that?"

"Yes, perfectly. Just don't get your hopes up about finding her, yet." She made a hopeless gesture. "It's going to be getting dark soon. Why don't you come to my house for the evening? You can leave my number with the police." Alison reached for Blake's hand. "It will be better for you."

"If it's all the same, I'd rather stay near home base, just in case, well . . . in case she comes home on her own."

"If you'd rather, but if you should change your mind . . ." Her words trailed off. Better to let him do as he wished. Some day she'd learn to stop meddling in other people's affairs.

They drove in silence back to his place, where she'd left her car earlier that morning.

"Call me as soon as you hear anything," Alison said, reaching for the door handle. Blake made a move toward her, pulled her into his arms and just held her there. His jawline was rough to the touch. He kissed her quickly and released her. "Drive safely," he said.

He watched as she got into her car and drove off. Entering his house, he immediately checked the answering machine for any messages. Nothing. Nothing at all.

Alison was exhausted, mentally and physically. But she knew her family had to be cared for. Tomorrow she'd take Willy home. Hopefully, by then there would be some word on Sondra. Pulling her cape about her, she hurried up the brick walk. The temperature had dropped well below freezing, and the falling snow had already covered the path.

Alison's concern for Sondra's whereabouts was answered the moment she opened the door. There on the couch, tears streaming down her pale cheeks, was Blake's daughter.

Chapter Nine

Oh, Mrs. Sherwood!'' Sondra gasped between sobs.

Alison flew to her side, put a comforting arm around the girl and softly said, "You're all right now."

Marge, who was on the other side of her, murmured, "She just got here, and I'm afraid we haven't been able to make much sense of what she's said. Something about some man dumping her out on Route 50."

Willy edged forward. "It was that Freedley boy, wasn't it?" Peter and Eric pressed forward, their eyes practically popping out of their heads.

But it was Robin who said in clear, accusatory tones, "Fred Freedley hangs around the school yard and sells pills!"

"I didn't know about the pills," Sondra gulped. "But he was nice to me...and when father threatened to put me in boarding school...I knew I wouldn't see him anymore. But last night—we didn't do anything. He wanted to, but..." Seeing the boys' curiosity, she stopped, her lips trembling as still more tears tracked dark paths down her cheeks.

"You don't need to talk just yet." Alison adjusted some pillows behind the teenager. "Why don't you rest, and I'll give your father a call."

"No!" The girl shot forward. "He doesn't want me around, and I don't want him to know where I am! He hates me."

"Oh, no. He doesn't," Alison contradicted. "He loves you. I know it may not look that way now, but he's been sick with worry."

"If he worried so about me, why did he want to send me to boarding school?" Sondra absently brushed tears from her face.

"It's because of creeps like Freedley!" Willy unexpectedly answered as he sat on the edge of the couch. "Also 'cause of the clothes you wear."

"*He* likes them on *his* girlfriends," Sondra sniffed, regaining some of her composure. She was obviously quite pleased with her snug jeans and tight red sweater.

Alison wished she could send all the children to the family room while she talked with Sondra, but this was not to be. Her three had plopped on the floor and were avidly watching Sondra as if she were a featured guest on Johnny Carson's show! And it was obvious wild horses couldn't budge Willy, who puffed up his chest, and in response to Sondra's remark, said, "You don't see Dad hanging out with those kind of women now, do you?"

"I don't care what he does anymore! Besides, Fred liked the way I dressed . . ." Her voice trailed off as a fresh supply of tears seemed imminent.

"So where's Fred now?" her brother pressed with disarming frankness.

Sondra let out a sob and flung herself back on the pillows. All the children leaned forward, spellbound.

Alison gently brushed a lock of auburn hair that had fallen across Sondra's eyes. "Did Fred hurt you?" she asked after a moment.

"He didn't beat me up or anything," the teen managed between tears. "He said we'd go south. I dunno what we were going to do when we got there. I don't think he knew, either. And when we were a few miles out of town, he just stopped the car and told me to get out." She paused, her lips trembling, and shook her head. "When I wouldn't get out, he . . . he . . . pushed me right onto Route 50! And so I spent the night at my friend Molly's house—we didn't tell her mother what happened—and then I came here. I hope it's all right."

"Of course it is," Alison reassured her as Marge appeared with steaming bowls of soup on a large tray.

Carefully Marge set it down on the coffee table. "You'll feel much better after you eat, child. In fact, I think we'll all benefit."

"Thanks," Sondra said, reaching for a bowl. "You all are really nice. I didn't know where else to go." She stared into the soup and slowly dipped her spoon into it.

"Despite what you think, your father *will* be relieved to know you're safe." Alison rose and quickly crossed to the kitchen. At the door, she added with a reassuring smile, "If you like, I'll ask him if you can stay here for a few days. After all it's midsemester break."

"Oh, I'd like that so much!" Sondra's eyes danced with unexpected light, only to darken quickly. "He doesn't want me around, that's for sure."

Alison started to contradict her but thought better of it. At least Sondra was all right, and that was what mattered.

A reconciliation with her father would take time, but Alison was determined to make it happen.

Blake answered on the first ring, his voice tense and edgy.

"She's here, Blake!"

"I'll be right over!" He hung up before she could tell him how Sondra was feeling. Alison dialed back immediately. He could ruin everything if he showed up now! His daughter was at least willing to trust another adult. His appearance now might well put that in jeopardy. She let it ring fifteen times, reluctantly depressed the receiver button and dialed the police. They thanked Alison for news of Sondra's whereabouts and said they'd come by the following morning to get a statement from her and her father.

Returning to the living room, she saw Sondra was finishing her soup and was looking much more relaxed. Her eyes flew up and met Alison's. She looked both expectant and fearful.

"What . . . what did my father say?"

"I'm afraid he hung up before I had a chance to tell him anything. He's on his way over here, but—" Alison sat on the couch and took hold of Sondra's hand "—don't worry about a thing. What I said still stands. In fact, I think it really would be a good thing for you to spend some time here." She smiled at her children. "You get along so well with Robin and the boys. And I'll take some time off from work and we'll do fun things. You'd like that, wouldn't you?"

"Sure." Sondra's voice sounded troubled. "But my father might not go along with it. He might even—"

"You let me handle your dad, okay?" Silently Alison wondered just how she would accomplish this but gave the girl a reassuring smile.

"That'll be fun, Sondra!" Robin chimed in, her blue eyes gleaming. "We can go shopping and do all kinds of things!"

"Yeah," the teenager agreed. She turned to Alison. "I'd sure like to go to the art-supply store in Georgetown."

"We'll stop there first. I need to get a few things myself."

"You sure you can take that time off from work, Mrs. Sherwood?"

"I'll make it a long lunch hour." Alison retrieved her soup bowl, and in between sips of lukewarm soup, said, "I understand from your dad that you're a really good artist, that you got an A in Drawing."

"Father said that?"

"Yes, he did. He's quite proud of you."

"You're just saying that. He doesn't even notice me." She tossed her head with a studied air, and again Alison was reminded of the afternoon soaps.

"You're wrong, Sondra. He's very concerned about you." Alison reached for her hand and gave it a squeeze. "But let's not worry about that. Why don't we write out a schedule for next week. You know, 'Zoo on Tuesday, shopping on Wednesday.' That sort of thing."

"Shopping!" the girl echoed. "Oh, that would be great. Do you suppose we could go to a fashion show?"

"I don't see why not." Alison rose and crossed to her rolltop desk. "I've got a catalogue in here somewhere." Quickly she located it and flipped through. "Looks like we're in luck. Neiman's has a lunchtime show this coming Thursday." Casually Alison placed the catalogue on the coffee table. "Why don't you and Robin look through it while Marge and I do the dishes." She nodded in her mother's direction, picked up the tray and started for the kitchen. Both girls pounced on the catalogue. The boys made disgruntled sounds about "silly girls" and tromped out of the room.

Ten minutes later Blake arrived. "Thank God, Sondra!" He made a move toward her, but checked himself and stood awkwardly at the door. There was so much he wanted to say to her, but the words wouldn't come. What *did* trouble him was the defiant look on her face.

"I'm all right, Father," she said at last. "But I don't want to come home," she added breathlessly. "Not yet, at least."

Alison appeared in the kitchen doorway, a tea towel in her hand. "Blake, I thought she could stay with us for a few days." She sent him an imploring look over his daughter's head, then crossed the room and said, "We've some warm soup in the kitchen. Why don't you come have some?"

"I'd like to talk with my daughter," he heard himself say in a sharp tone. "Well, Sondra?" She avoided his eyes and muttered a response that further annoyed him.

"You know, I am your father." He felt his hands clench and unclench as he strode into the room, stopping a few feet from where Sondra and Robin sat. This wasn't going the way he'd planned it, but that shouldn't have surprised him. A slow burn crept up his neck. "I think you have some explaining to do, young lady."

"Why do you always call me 'young lady'?" She looked up from the catalogue and quickly down again. Robin sat stock-still, her eyes glued to the page in feigned fascination.

Suddenly Blake felt like a bully. He backed off. Whatever explanation Sondra had, he'd have to get from Alison. He supposed it could wait. His daughter was safe and that's what counted. Being head of a multimillion-dollar business didn't mean that much after all. He was a failure at what mattered: being a father.

"I'd like to talk to you in the kitchen, Alison," he said in a voice he barely recognized.

"Good idea," Alison agreed. Marge, who was wiping down the stove, gave a cheery hello as they entered and discreetly left the room.

"Sondra's been through a lot," Alison began. With a sigh, she settled into a chair and poured out the remains of some tea into two cups. "Have a seat." She gestured towards a chair. "Afraid this is lukewarm. I'll heat it up if you like."

Blake waved away the offer and, sinking into the indicated chair, said, "What happened?"

Alison couldn't remember ever seeing him look so utterly devastated, as if the past twenty-four hours had aged him ten years. "Blake, Sondra will come around, and I'm not saying you're to blame, but you should ease off a little. Forgive me for being so frank." She shrugged. "It's really none of my business."

"What did happen to her?" Blake repeated.

"The police were right, Sondra *did* run away." Quickly she added, "I called and let them know she had turned up here. They're coming by tomorrow morning to question you both."

"My daughter, a runaway."

"Oh, Blake, it's not because she doesn't love you, but because she thinks you don't love her."

"But that's ridiculous," he protested. "Maybe I don't always show it, but I care very much for her welfare. Why, that was the reason for the boarding school."

"Yes, and that was why she ran off," Alison said. "Seems she found someone at school who drove her out of town."

"Who?" The word exploded from his mouth.

"A boy in her class. Don't worry, nothing happened. He chickened out and left her on Route 50, and she ultimately made her way back here—unharmed, but shaken up, to say the least. I don't think she'll be taking off again." Alison hesitated, wondering just how much she should tell him about Fred Freedley. The boy's conduct had to be reported to the school authorities, and it would look very strange if Alison handled the affair. There was no avoiding it; Blake would have to be told at least part of the story. She took a sustaining gulp of tea and, to her surprise, managed to convey just enough of the incident without revealing too much. Blake's thoughts were on Sondra's well-being, and taking a shotgun to Fred Freedley was not uppermost in his mind, though he assured Alison that the incident would be handled.

Gingerly Alison brought up the possibility of Sondra spending part of her midsemester break with them, pointing out how enjoyable it would be for the girl to be with Robin and the boys. Far better than with the Fred Freedleys of the world, though this last was left unsaid.

Absently Blake ran his fingers through his hair. "If it's what Sondra wants, then yes, I suppose it's better than the undeclared war we'd wage." A twisted smile settled on his face. "Parenting is obviously not my strong suit."

"It's tough being a single parent, I know."

"Yes, but at least you do an admirable job. I don't see your kids hanging out in bars or running off."

"Robin's a bit young," Alison said with a much-needed touch of humor. "As for the boys, take it from me, they're a handful."

"It's somehow different with a father and daughter, and since Ginny died it's been a struggle."

"I know, but, Blake, remember that underneath her pain, I know Sondra loves you." Alison reached across the table and touched his hand. "How could it be otherwise?"

He looked at her and his smile flashed on like a light. "Thanks, Eskimo."

Everything went like clockwork the following morning: Blake and the police, good to their word, appeared simultaneously. The officers briefly questioned Sondra and Blake, then left. The only awkwardness occurred between father and daughter.

After he left Alison's, Blake navigated the nightmarish traffic across Key Bridge. A tow truck had slid on the ice, barely missing several cars, and the ensuing jam and honking horns was one more irritant in a not-too-promising morning. Had it only been yesterday that he and Alison had combed the malls for Sondra? And now she was safe but uncommunicative, as far as he was concerned. With Alison, it was different. Sondra had formed a surprising attachment to her. If anyone could work wonders on his daughter, it would be Alison. Maneuvering around a stalled car, Blake thought about some of her suggestions. Perhaps putting Sondra in a boarding school *wasn't* such a good idea. But if not that, what? It was a pretty sorry state of affairs when the president of Camelot Enterprises couldn't even figure out how to handle his domestic crisis. Alison would have some ideas, and yet she was doing so much for him already. If only he could find a way to repay her.

By the time he got to the office, an idea had begun to germinate. He could set everything up—Alison need never know, but at least he'd feel he had done something. Maybe he didn't always express his deepest feelings, but his power and position did reap their rewards. He pushed the intercom button and asked McGee to get a certain party on the line. With his fingers steepled before him, he leaned back and waited. Calling in your debts was just one of the fringe benefits of power.

Meanwhile Alison and Robin watched as one of Neiman's cosmeticians gave Sondra a consultation. Every ounce of dime store makeup was removed. This was followed by a thick clay mask that sent both Robin and the teenager into giggles.

"No, no!" the beautician admonished as she smoothed the clay over Sondra's face. "You must not move a muscle." Deftly she removed all traces of clay from her long fingers. Alison envied those tapering pink nails. But then like all beauticians advertising their products, she looked the part of perfection as she moved in a cloud of softly perfumed air.

Once the mask was removed, the cosmetician showed Sondra how to cleanse and moisturize her skin. This was followed by a lesson in makeup application that included a light foundation, a hint of blusher and a touch of mascara. Naturally the woman also tried to sell Alison a variety of creams, but she stood firm. She did, however, buy some pink nail polish and bubble bath for Robin.

"How come you didn't get your face done?" Sondra asked as they started for the Young Misses department.

"We would have been here another hour, besides I have a line of makeup I like." She didn't add that it was a haphazard array that would have horrified the beautician. For Sondra, though, the little kit they'd purchased was a perfect boost for her self-esteem. Alison smiled at the girl, noting how proudly she held herself and how firmly she gripped her package.

An hour later they left the Young Misses department with a shopping bag stuffed with the latest fashions for both girls. For Sondra this included a slim-line pair of jeans, two cotton blouses in candy-cane stripes, a denim jumper and a drop-waist party dress in apricot silk. Surprisingly Robin didn't seem to mind coming out on the short end of the stick, and she chattered ecstatically about how beautiful her friend Sondra looked. The *I Love Cats* sweatshirt Alison got her daughter seemed to balance things out nicely.

Since it was lunchtime, they stopped at the same taco shop that she and Blake had eaten in the day before. Sondra very pointedly asked the waitress for a vegetarian burrito, and an iced tea instead of her usual cola. With youthful candor she said, "I want to be in as good shape as you when I'm your age!"

"I'm not exactly a relic, Sondra, but thanks for the compliment," Alison said as she turned to the waitress and gave her order.

"Yeah, but you should see some of the women Father used to take out. They looked a lot older than you." Abruptly she clapped her hand over her mouth, slowly let it slide down and added sheepishly, "He doesn't go out with *them* anymore!" Gathering her courage, she continued, "But one of them had lots of wrinkles and she was only twenty-five. I bet it comes from junk food. She wore a leopard coat, too!" With a sigh Sondra pulled her napkin into her lap. "I don't know why I ever wanted to look like her!"

"Perhaps you saw her as glamorous," Alison offered as an unpleasant vision of a woman in a leopard coat appeared.

Robin, who'd been silent until then, said, "Well, Mom is way over twenty-five, and she's still glamorous!"

"Fer sure," Sondra agreed, and turned to Alison. "And you're much nicer than any of the ladies Father used to see."

Alison smiled at Sondra's observation. The reeducation of Blake's daughter was going a lot faster than she'd originally thought, and it was certainly not without its lighter moments.

"That was some lunch hour you had!" Ingrid remarked as Alison returned to the office.

"I know! I know!" She laughed. "But I assure you it's all for a good cause, and we're practically finished Valentino's Pleasure." Casually riffling through papers on her desk, she asked, "How did Mrs. Grant's solarium turn out?"

"She was so pleased that she wants to redecorate the upstairs bedrooms. All six of them. In fact, as soon as I finish these statements I'm heading over there." Ingrid paused by the door. "From the looks of things, it's going to be a profitable spring!"

"We might just have to hire another assistant," Alison said gaily. "Who knows, we might become millionaires yet," she added on a laugh as the phone rang. A low voice at the other end grumbled, and immediately Alison snapped to attention, and, gripping the receiver as if it were a lifeline, she slowly sank into her chair.

The conversation lasted all of three minutes. "I don't believe it," she murmured as she hung up.

"Try enlightening me," Ingrid suggested.

"That was Martin Acheson!"

"The producer of *Hello America*?"

"Right, the TV morning talk show!" Alison shot from her chair in a burst of nervous energy. "He wants me as a guest."

"What?"

"It's crazy, but it seems his wife was in Georgetown last week and noticed the new awning on Valentino's—or rather My Lady's Chamber. She decided to go in, fell in love with the new decor, and was so excited that she asked the name of the designer. Voilà! Mr. Acheson just happens to be doing a special, *The New Georgetown Entrepreneurs*. Do you know what this will mean?"

Ingrid excitedly gave her friend and partner a hug. "It means, Ms. Sherwood, that we might hire several assistants after all and move to a larger space."

"Whoa!" Alison took a deep breath. "Let's not count our chickens before they hatch."

"We can make one hell of an omelet!" Ingrid countered. "You'd be sensational on TV." Stepping back, she gave Alison a critical look. "Have your hair done and wear something gorgeous and—"

"Hey, Ingrid, not so fast!" She gave a pat to her dark upswept hair and added, "I'm going as I am, though a new outfit might be nice. And—" she crossed to her drafting board "—some of Valentino's renderings."

"Did this Martin Acheson have a date in mind? I mean, the man must be pretty sure of himself to assume you'd—"

"Yes, to both questions," Alison mumbled as she continued to eye her renderings.

"So when are you scheduled to appear?" Ingrid prodded.

Alison flashed her a smile and slipped the sketches into a portfolio. "Would you believe this Friday? They plan months in advance, but their scheduled guest canceled at the last moment." On an intake of breath she exclaimed, "Oh, Lord, I'd better call Blake!" As she passed Ingrid, she whispered, "Pinch me."

Chapter Ten

There's more good news, too," Alison said. "I think Sondra really *is* on the mend. We just need to give her time."

"Have you thought of applying for sainthood?" After a moment, he huskily added, "Scratch that, and let's take the rest of the day off and make mad passionate love." He was teasing, but she knew he'd take her up on it in a minute if she agreed.

"We have to stop meeting like this," she parried back, feeling her heart skip a beat and wondering dizzily how she was going to get through the rest of the day.

"Are you suggesting I make an honest woman of you? Because I'm beginning to think that's the only way we'll have some time alone." Blake was amazed at the sudden turn the conversation was taking. This was not what he'd intended. Yes, he wanted Alison, more than any other woman, but the words were coming out all wrong.

Before he had a chance to add anything, Alison said teasingly, "Do you usually make such propositions on the phone?"

"If you can wait till Thursday, I'll do it on bended knee," Blake said in a voice that surprised him. Then recklessly he continued, "I've done a lot of thinking, Alison, and you and the kids mean more to me than anything else. I know I've made some pretty bad mistakes, but I'm learning." He heard his ragged intake of breath as if it were someone else. But dammit, she *did* mean the world to him! "Listen, a business deal in Chicago came up this morning, and I'm going to have to fly out this afternoon. Could you keep Willy for a few nights? When I get back we'll talk ... well, more than talk. But there's so much I need to tell you, it's just that it's hard for me."

"I know, Blake. Yes, I'll be happy to take care of Willy. You'll be back before the *Hello America* interview, won't you?"

"Count on it. We'll go out and celebrate—bended knee and all. We'll make it an early evening so you'll be fresh for your TV appearance." Blake paused and took a breath. He'd laid his cards on the table without even knowing the hand. "Until Thursday then."

After the disconnection Alison sat holding the receiver. There was so much more she wanted to say: to finally confess her love for him, to tell him how much he meant to her. Instead, she'd said goodbye. She had spent her entire life without knowing Blake McLaughlin, and now a three-day separation suddenly seemed eternal.

The rest of the afternoon dragged by, but another call from Martin Acheson gave her a shot of adrenaline. Carolina Webster, the MC for the talk show, wanted to meet with her and get some interview questions set up beforehand. Would lunch tomorrow be too soon? Not at all, Alison replied, she'd be delighted.

When Alison told Marge and the kids about the interview, they buzzed about her as if she were a queen bee. Sally Jean, hearing the commotion, appeared from the kitchen.

"*You* are going to be on *Hello America*?" Sally Jean asked, practically genuflecting. Dog had come up behind her and was gently nosing her palm for a treat. Alison thought somewhat distractedly how things had changed in the past week.

"Yes, Sally Jean. It seems the producer's wife walked into the new Valentino's and was impressed." Alison shrugged her shoulder expressively. "I must admit I find it all a bit surprising. Maybe I have a fairy godmother looking out for me."

Robin nodded. "Just like Cinderella. Ooh, I can't wait till all my friends at school find out!"

"So, Mom," Pete cut in, "are you gonna be making big bucks now?" Robin and Eric chorused this.

"Children, children!" Marge swept forward. "You would think we were living in the arms of poverty. This is merely one more step in your mother's future, and it was all in that reading I did for her." She puffed herself up. "You *do* remember my saying that your career and love prospects would take a definite swing for the better, don't you?"

"And I thought it was just mother-love talking!" Alison responded.

"Well, I sure could use another computer," Pete slipped in.

Eric, lounging near the fireplace with his thumbs hooked in his belt, added, "We could even move to a bigger house."

"You boys shall move to the den!" Marge clapped her hands for effect. "The girls may stay." Robin and Sondra exchanged gleeful looks.

"Sissy girls," Eric muttered as he purposely scuffed his running shoes across the Oriental rug.

Sally Jean seemed rooted to the spot. "I've never known a celebrity."

"Heavens, I'm *not* a celebrity. This is just PR for my business," Alison said on a laugh.

"And about time." Marge waved her hands regally and headed for the bookshelves that surrounded the fireplace. "Sally Jean, do sit down and have a glass of dandelion wine with us."

"My guru—that is, my ex-guru," Sally Jean began, "said that celebrities were on the lost path and that they would be weighed down with their possessions." The girl slowly sank onto the Victorian love seat as if she were throwing her lot in with the materialists. Carelessly she ran her hand across the velvet fabric. "Of course, that was before he was arrested for income tax evasion."

"Just like Al Capone!" Marge sang out as she placed the crystal decanter of wine on the coffee table. "Robin, why don't you and Sondra get some juice from the kitchen, and bring out the rice biscuits."

"I don't know much about Al Capone, but my ex-guru had a whole lot of valuable stuff in Hyattsville."

"Hyattsville." Marge wrinkled her nose as if she'd just smelled something rotten. "It's positively at the end of the earth. Ah, but then Guru Shikti-whatever was obviously not in total possession." She tapped her head for emphasis, poured out the wine and handed it around. It was dreadful stuff, but Alison had never had the heart to tell her.

"To your success!" Marge proclaimed, raising her glass.

Sally Jean echoed the sentiment and continued, "My ex-guru was all wrong about celebrities. I've never been happier in my life!" She took a healthy slug of wine and beamed her approval. She obviously liked the wine, but not her ex-guru from Hyattsville.

"And we are delighted with you," Marge assured her. "Why, you're a part of the family, and *should* we get a larger place, you could certainly move in with us!"

Alison wasn't sure about that, but she merely smiled and took a sip of the dandelion wine, her thoughts drifting back to her conversation with Blake. Had he really meant what he said? Marriage? When he returned Thursday she'd find out. Little did she know, however, the revelations that were in store for her.

Her luncheon the following day with Carolina Webster went off without a hitch. The interviewer was as smooth as glass and very practiced at her craft of getting into another's shoes. Slim, blond and chic, the media called her the Barbara Walters of the daytime talk show.

"Tell me your opinion of Mr. McLaughlin," she flung out as they were finishing up their peach melbas.

"Well, if it weren't for him, I wouldn't have redecorated Valentino's, and I suppose you wouldn't be interviewing me." She tried to sound professional and yet light. Putting down her spoon, she leaned forward and said, "He's been wonderful to work for. We've been in perfect agreement on everything." So what if she extended the truth a bit?

"My question, Ms. Sherwood, was off the record, if you know what I mean." Her voice, suddenly hushed, encouraged confidences, but her eyes, a cool gray and as unreadable as stones, were not to be trusted.

"I know so little of Mr. McLaughlin." Now she was lying barefaced, and over a melting peach melba, at that.

Carolina gave an indolent shrug of her silk-clad shoulders. "I just thought perhaps, being as he is the most eligible, not to mention wealthy *and* successful bachelor on the east coast..." She purposefully let her sentence trail off and, with a nod of her perfectly coiffed head, silently motioned for coffee.

Suddenly Alison had a funny feeling about this interview. Carolina Webster was known for delving deeper than most interviewers, and always with a lovely smile. Her instincts were good, Alison was certain of that, and having been a reporter for *The Washington Post* before hosting the *Hello America* show, Carolina knew how to deliver what the people wanted. Her show wasn't popular for nothing.

They didn't linger over coffee. Carolina had gotten what she needed, and with a flourish she signed for the check and smiled the smile that didn't quite reach her eyes.

No sooner had Alison come in the door that evening than Marge fluttered forward, wringing her hands like a heroine from a silent film. The smell of burned kidney beans filled the air.

"Oh, my dear, dear Alison!" the flustered Marge began in her highest register. With a dramatic backhand gesture, as if she were about to deliver an opening tennis shot, she indicated the man on the love seat, who immediately jackknifed forward, all six foot three of him. One large hand gripped a worn Stetson, the other sprang out in greeting.

"Clem North's the name, ma'am, but I come from the South, as I guess you gathered." His smile displayed buck teeth and several gold crowns. He swallowed and his

Adam's apple bobbed. "I'm the Sagittarian." This announcement only confused Alison more.

"Well, I'm a Leo," she said, trying to catch on. "And a very hungry one, too."

"Oh, dear. Sally Jean and I got to talking with Clem, and we burned the bean casserole and the rice." She looked at the ceiling for celestial guidance. "And the hijiki, too, but there's some salad, and Sally's gone to the 7-Eleven."

"Hijiki?" The man from down South looked puzzled. "Sounds foreign to me."

"Well, it is," Marge said as if confessing a sin. "Japanese."

"Now why'd you want to go and eat Japanese food when what we got right here is plenty good. You take barbeque, for instance," Clem suggested.

"I'd rather not." Marge wrinkled her nose and hastily poured more wine into the man's glass. "Please, do make yourself comfy while Alison and I just see what else we can do about dinner."

"Sure thing, but don't worry about that funny-sounding stuff." He nodded his head and folded his angular body onto the love seat.

"Mother," Alison began in hushed tones as they entered the kitchen, "where did you dig that one up, and what is he doing here?"

"Oh, dear, dear, dear. It's such a muddle. Thank God the children aren't here to further confuse things." She hurried on, "Do you remember my telling you some months ago that the . . . um—" she cleared her throat "—the love of your life would be showing up? Well . . ."

"Surely that's not him. I mean, really, Mother." Alison swung the refrigerator door open and looked in vain at the near-empty shelves.

"We've got some escarole and tofu." Marge pulled them off the shelves. "Oh, my, the tofu does look a bit pink."

"About Rhett Butler—"

Marge gave her daughter a quelling look as she dumped the tofu down the garbage disposal. "You needn't be sarcastic. He's really quite sweet."

"I didn't say he wasn't, but if you've done what I think you've done."

"Well, yes and no." Marge quickly rinsed the escarole. "The Astro Match Service guarantees that they will find your soul mate. Oh, not right away, but within three years, and I thought—"

"That I needed some help in finding Mr. Right?"

"Yes." She gave a vigorous shake to the wilted lettuce and placed it on the drain board. "But after we explain to him that—"

"We?" Alison grabbed a knife and began chopping carrots.

"*I* will—you know—tell him that you've been spoken for." Marge gave her daughter a crafty look.

"You sound positively medieval. You've been reading more romances, haven't you?" She popped a carrot slice into her mouth.

"Let me explain how all this happened," Marge went on, ignoring the gibe. "I took out an advertisement and screened the first responses. Most of them were all wrong for you. Then after a while nothing came, and I frankly forgot. That is, until Mr. North showed up." Tearing the lettuce, she hastily put it into the salad bowl.

"No letter from him?"

"Oh, I simply can't remember.... There might have been. Yes, I think he did write, but that was way back in December, and you know how it is at Christmas. I must have put it aside with the cards. Of course, I didn't tell our Mr. North that."

"Mother, he is not 'our' Mr. North!" Alison dumped the carrots on top of the escarole.

"You must admit, it *is* a nice name."

"Charming. Now, let's take this salad out there and . . . and tell Mr. North—"

"He's not the one. Tell him that over an escarole-and-carrot salad?"

"We'll put some dressing on it, and give him some more wine."

"Oh, not so much on an empty stomach. I'm surprised at you, Alison. By the way, how did your luncheon go?"

"Okay, I suppose, but she got a little too personal."

"That's her job. Hedda Hopper was good at that sort of thing, too." Marge held up the salad dressing bottle and muttered, "I suppose this will be enough."

"Still, Carolina Webster seemed more interested in my relationship with Blake than in my work."

"He *is* a well-known bachelor, so naturally—"

Alison sent her mother a quelling glare. "This looks naked," she remarked, changing the subject.

"We can round it out when Sally Jean gets back from the 7-Eleven."

"I can't believe you sent her to that haven of junk food," Alison said on a laugh as she entered the dining room.

"Our Mr. North won't notice. He's quite used to microwaved burritos, I'm sure."

Alison forgot what she was about to say. There in front of her was the answer. Sally Jean had returned from the 7-Eleven and was presently perched on the arm of Marge's Queen Anne wing chair, practically drooling into Mr. North's lap. He seemed equally taken with her, and a more incongruous pair Alison had never seen. Jack Sprat and his wife. Alison hated to interrupt the interlude, but she was ready to eat the dining room table!

"Were you able to find vegetarian burritos?" she asked, depositing the salad on the table. It looked desperately lonely.

"Oh, yes!" Sally Jean's eyes flew up, all dewy and sparkling. "Would you believe Mr. North and I—"

"Please call me Clem." His drawl was thick enough to spread.

"Clem—that Clem and I come from the same neck of the woods."

Alison refrained from saying that she would believe anything. Instead she added saccharine to the sugar. "Why, isn't that something." Her stomach growled and she quickly said, "I'm sure Clem's hungry, so—"

Sally Jean leapt from the chair. "I didn't even think of that!" She proudly patted her midsection. "I've been on a diet these past two weeks. Lost fifteen pounds, so I try not to think of food." She slanted an approval-seeking grin in Clem's direction.

"Hell, I think you look just fine the way you are. Okay for a man to be all bone, but not for a lady." Once again he displayed the prominent teeth and gold work. There was an awful lot of it, and, as Alison continued a surreptitious inspection of their Mr. North, she noticed quantities of turquoise-and-silver jewelry. A suede coat was carelessly tossed to one side, and his long legs were encased in matching pants. The leather boots appeared to be hand tooled. Oil, Alison thought. He must be the answer to Sally Jean's affirmation on the refrigerator door. "I am now attracting my perfect mate."

"I'll eat anything, so long's it ain't crawling," Clem said as he flipped one of Marge's antique dining room chairs around and straddled it like a horse.

Alison caught her mother's eye. She was obviously thinking the same thing. Guardedly, and in between bites of burrito, Alison studied the pair. He was too thin and too rich, and Sally Jean, in her bargain-basement outfit, was neither. It was a match made in heaven. He was from Texas, just like she was, just like Blake. Marge would surely have something later to say about their karma with Texans!

As the evening drew to a close, Alison noticed that Clem seemed ill at ease. His Adam's apple was traveling up and down his throat at an alarming rate.

"If I could have a word with you, private, ma'am," he said when Sally Jean disappeared into the kitchen. Marge took the hint and slipped out of the room, too.

"I expect this is going to come as a letdown, especially after my letter, but I feel I have to be honest with a fine lady like you." He leaned on the table and looked at her intently. "Now, I didn't come here under false pretenses. I figured that there might be something between you and me, even though I didn't get an answer to my letter. But, anyway, I have to tell you franklike, and, as you know, we Sagittarians have to spill our guts, even if it means a mess. But fact is, I think you ought to consider another man, 'cause I've taken to Sally Jean. Probably as we're from the same town and all." He pulled out a self-congratulatory cigar and fingered it lovingly.

"I appreciate your frankness." She considered telling him the truth, what she would have told him if he hadn't coughed up his confession first, but on second thought, she decided to let it ride. He probably had a fragile ego beneath all that silver and suede. She smiled her professional smile. "I'm sure there are other Sagittarians out there."

"That's the spirit!" He broke the cellophane off the cigar. "What I can't figure out is how a triple Pisces and a double Sagittarian with a moon in Taurus would get on so well. Then I'm new at this astrology business. Oil speculation is what I do best." As he stuck the cigar into his mouth, Alison noticed the star sapphire on his pinky. Yes, she expected he did real well in oil.

Alison had never known a rich Texan, and now two had popped into her life. Blake would have enjoyed the evening. He would have probably slipped into a drawl as thick as molasses. Blake... He'd be coming home on Thursday. They would celebrate, drink champagne, and he would go down on one knee. The image brought a smile to her lips. Clem and Blake, so different.

As the evening drew to a close, the children—stuffed with birthday cake—returned from their friend's party, and Sally Jean and Clem made plans for the rest of the week. What a day it had been!

Much later, the house lay quiet. The children and the pets were tucked in for the night, and Alison lay in bed, watching the play of light and shadow on the ceiling and wondering what it would be like waking up next to Blake McLaughlin. A little thrill went through her, and she squeezed her eyes shut and pretended he was beside her. "Soon, soon," she sighed.

The next two days passed in frenzied activity. At work Alison was suddenly deluged with clients. A small piece had appeared in the *Post*'s TV section about Carolina Webster's guest *The chic up-and-coming designer Alison O'Shaunnessey Sherwood*. Good God, where did they dig up her maiden name?

"Is this what they call the cutting edge?" Alison moaned as she flipped through her calender. "The Chumleys want a three-room doghouse with Chippendale couches for their Great Danes?"

"Don't laugh," Ingrid admonished, placing the day's mail on her desk. "We're in the fast lane now."

"But what's with these Chumleys?"

"Oh, that order came while you were on the phone with Gramercy Restaurant. I guess Chip and Henriette Chumley want to have a château for their pooches. That matches their 'little' estate."

"Did you explain we're not architects?" Alison asked as she tossed her engagement calendar to one side.

"Oh, the château's already in place. They just want wallpaper and furnishings." Ingrid's eyes sparkled. "And since they're willing to pay top dollar, who are we to argue?"

"I'm not even sure I know what top dollar is anymore."

"I do. Never fear." Ingrid headed for the door, paused and turned around. "It's just a miniature château. Sort of a combination dollhouse and small cottage."

"Snow White and the Seven Dwarfs with crawl space, I presume?" Alison asked with a laugh.

"I presume. This is the price of fame, Ms. Sherwood. Every front has its back," was Ingrid's parting shot as she sailed out the door only to reappear minutes later. "Look who's here!"

Blake strode forward. "One of the Seven Dwarfs!" he growled as he enfolded Alison in a bear hug.

"Oh, Blake, you wouldn't believe what these past three days have been like!" Her voice was muffled in the chilly lapel of his cashmere coat. He smelled of a woodsy cologne. When his mouth descended to hers, she tasted snowflakes and a winter afternoon, yet it warmed her through and through.

"I've missed you so," she said at last, looking into his jet-black eyes that smoldered just for her.

"And I, you, my little Eskimo." He stepped back. "Yes, you look like you need a little of this. You, too, Ingrid." He held up a bottle of Moët champagne. "Any crystal lying around?"

"How about Dixie cups?" Alison asked, pulling several from her desk drawer.

"Fine, fine." Blake shrugged out of his coat, laid it over a chair and popped the cork out of the champagne.

"You always get the best, don't you?" Alison quickly held the cups out. Even so, the bubbles frothed over the edge. They all laughed and touched cups.

"So you've had a busy three days?" Blake said as he lowered himself into a chair.

"Insane and wonderful, and I may never have to worry about paying bills again!" She winked at Ingrid as she eased herself onto a stool. Ingrid, as usual, preferred the edge of Alison's desk.

Blake sipped thoughtfully at his champagne. "Good fairy been sprinkling gold dust on you?"

"We were doing all right before, but now we're swamped with clients, and all because of the upcoming TV interview."

"You ready for that?" he casually asked as he filled the small cups again.

"As ready as I'll ever be. I met Carolina Webster for lunch. She's quite an inquisitive person."

"That's why she gets almost a million a year. Ah, you'll be great, Eskimo! And this exposure will double your business."

"We'll probably have to move," Ingrid said with a sigh, looking at the high-ceilinged room. "Into a larger place, more personnel, bigger reception area, and that will mean more velvet love seats. It can go on and on."

"Whoa," Alison pleaded. "You're as bad as Mom and the kids. They're all set to move into Buckingham Palace! Let's just take one day at a time."

As they finished up the champagne, Alison told Blake about the Chumleys' three-room dog château. This brought a chuckle to his lips. They went on to talk about his children, and he was pleased to learn that Sondra had mentioned him several times.

"She's going to have to move back home," Blake told Alison later as they stopped off at his house. "Because you and I are going to be living together. I was serious about the bended knee routine." Pulling into his driveway, he added, "I'm not very good with words."

Alison felt her face grow flushed, and very quietly she said, "You? The president of Camelot, at a loss for words?" She knew what he meant, that he had trouble expressing his deeper emotions, and this confession on his part seemed to leave *her* speechless. This man was talking about marriage, and all Alison could do was mumble inanities.

"Yes," he said at last, "the big cheese has a hard time saying what he really means, but he's working on it. Come on in while I check my mail, then we'll get dinner at that Japanese restaurant you liked so much." He turned off the engine and without hesitation pulled her into his arms and began kissing her, lightly, teasingly, and then with mounting ardor. Abruptly he drew back and with mock severity said, "Look what you've reduced me to!"

"A little late-afternoon lust in the front seat?" she said, making no attempt to hide her own growing passion.

Deftly she slipped her hands inside his coat, and would have worked the buttons open if he hadn't captured her eager fingers in his own. Cupping her palms, he pressed kisses into them. A hot liquid fire surged through her veins. How quickly he aroused her. The slightest touch and she was ready for him. But today it was different, for he loved her, really loved her, and he wanted to marry her. All of Alison's dreams were coming true. She had both professional success and the man she so ardently desired. Nothing could change any of that. Or so she thought.

"Damn," Blake muttered as they entered the house. Pausing in the darkened hall, he tried several other light switches. "Looks like I've blown a fuse again."

"Again?"

"The wiring in these old houses leaves a lot to be desired." Reaching into his pocket, he pulled out matches, struck one and led Alison into the living room. Just as the match was going out, he managed to light two candles on the mantelpiece. He handed one to Alison and said, "Won't take me a minute to check out the fuse box. Make yourself comfy." He disappeared into the hall, his flickering shadow dancing on the walls.

Candle in hand, Alison moved toward the bay window that faced the street. Frost shimmered on the glass, and, outside, several trees stood like sentinels, their icy branches reaching upward to the cold and darkened sky. The half moon was slowly slipping into the cradle of bare limbs. The view was romantic and Alison felt slightly Gothic. Jane Eyre and the troubled Rochester came to mind but were quickly dismissed by two shrill rings of the phone and the answering machine flipping on. There was a beep, then a familiar voice.

"Acheson here. Where the hell are *you*? Calling in more favors? 'Cause, old boy, I think we're even now. Carolina had lunch with your gal. She was a real looker, but close-mouthed as hell when it came to chatting about our number one bachelor of the hour. Hell, you're too old for that kind of stuff, anyway. But I did what you asked, and she'll be none the wiser. Good publicity for that Valentino's bordello you bought. Signing off here." There was a click, and the red light on the machine began to flash.

Alison felt the color drain from her face at the realization of what she'd just heard. Blake had set the whole thing up! Good publicity for Valentino's, indeed! He had called in a favor with the top producer of WNBR. No wonder the man got everything he wanted. He bought and sold his way to the top, heedless of the people in his path. Marriage! Bended knee! How could he hand her a line like that? But then, hadn't he said from the beginning that he didn't make commitments? She should have believed him then. She was blinded by a sudden rush of tears that she dashed away with her hand. Taking a deep breath, she steadied her nerves. She set the candle down, reached into her purse and withdrew her business card and a pen. Hastily she wrote, "I'll do your Carolina Webster publicity, but that ends it!" So what if it was a dramatic gesture? At this point, nothing mattered except getting out before he returned.

She caught a cab on M Street, and in a shaky voice gave the driver her address. This was one of the days she'd walked to work. She'd been feeling so high, so elated at the thought of Blake's homecoming. Never again. The happiness they'd shared during these past two weeks had been counterfeit, and she had been as naive and gullible as a teenager. She wouldn't cry, either, even though the pain begged for release. Let him go back to the kind of women he really liked—the women in leopard coats!

February had never been Alison's favorite month.

That evening he called three times before finally appearing on the doorstep and refusing to budge.

"My dear, he'll freeze to death," her mother admonished as she returned to the kitchen where Alison was chopping vegetables with a vengeance.

"How can he?" She waved the knife dangerously. "He has ice for blood."

"I think you're a bit hard on him."

"Hard on *him*?" Disbelief rang in Alison's voice. "What about me? He went behind my back for his own gain!"

"We don't know that for sure." Marge sighed and turned to a pot of soup on the stove. "You surely don't intend to let him camp on the stoop all night. When Sally Jean and Clem return, they'll find it a little strange, too. Especially Sondra." Her eyebrows rose a fraction. "You don't want to undo all the good work you've done with the girl. Didn't you tell me she was speaking favorably of her father this morning?"

Alison made a face and admitted, "I suppose you're right. The sooner I see him, the better. I don't want to have a scene in front of Sondra." She scraped the onions into a sizzling wok. "But don't you dare ask him to dinner!"

"I'll leave that to you," Marge conceded as she exited.

Alison gave a pat to her upswept hair in an attempt to compose herself. Why couldn't he just take her note at face value? She'd made a clean break, and it felt as if her heart had been torn from her body. She'd managed to control herself in the cab, but once inside her own home, the tears had come in torrents. Thank God no one had been there.

Turning off the onions, Alison headed for the living room. She'd fix dinner after he left.

"Alison," Blake began as he crossed to meet her. Checking himself, he backed up a pace. "I know what you must be thinking, but everything can be explained." He was holding a rather pathetic bouquet of roses that he gingerly placed on the edge of the coffee table.

"Blake McLaughlin, I don't need an explanation. Your answering machine spoke for itself, or, should I say, Martin Acheson did." She pressed her lips into a tight line to keep them from trembling and, averting her eyes, stared at the thirsty roses. As she impulsively reached for them, his hand closed over hers, held it fast and drew her toward him. Against all will and reason, she felt her body ache for him.

"No," she said, pulling herself away. "I meant what I said in my note!"

The front door burst open, and Clem and Sally Jean tottered in singing "The Yellow Rose of Texas." A silver flask was clutched to Sally Jean's breast, and she hiccuped violently between the lyrics.

"We're three sheets to the wind." Clem drawled. Straightening himself, he took a cocky step toward Alison and Blake, who remained openmouthed at this unexpected interruption.

Clem fixed an unblinking eye on Alison. "You are one special woman, Ali."

"Ali?" Blake said softly, looking from the towering Texan to the woman beside him.

"Well, thank you, Clem, and now I'm sure you and Sally Jean will want to...to..." She made a weak gesture.

"Take a load off these tired legs," Sally Jean supplied as she plunked herself into a wing chair. "I haven't had three margaritas in a long time."

"Like I was saying, Ali, you made the ultimate sacrifice. But just look 'pon it as a star in your crown."

"Ultimate sacrifice?" Alison was momentarily non-plussed by the declaration.

"Me! Why I know you had your heart set on our rela-tionship. It was made in astrology heaven, and I didn't travel all these miles for nothing." He was speaking slowly now, making sure every word was distinct.

"Let me get this straight," Blake said, stepping for-ward. "You're saying you came up here from—"

"Texas, honey, Texas," Sally Jean offered.

"Texas." Blake made it sound contagious. "And you and Ms. Sherwood had been corresponding in a sort of...lonely hearts club?"

"Lonely hearts from the Lone Star State," Clem an-swered as he threw out his chest. "Yep. Me and Ms. Sher-wood was on real good terms, had a kinda agreement."

Alison sputtered, but nothing intelligible came out. Blake eyed her curiously and said, "Go on."

"Well, I knew she was broke up about the fact I got sweet on Sally Jean. But let's face it, you gotta follow your heart, and frankly when you got a load of greenbacks, you gotta realize it makes you more appealing. Now Sally Jean here, she don't need no money, but Alison musta been in a pretty bad way, I reckon, when she first put the personal in the Astro Match Service."

"Very interesting." Blake strode for the door, turned around abruptly and said, "Ms. Sherwood doesn't seem to need anyone these days, but then her business is boom-ing."

Sally Jean, who had drifted into a stupor, roused her-self to add, "Alison's a c'lebrity."

"Yes, it appears she is." Blake turned to face Alison. "If it's not too much trouble, I'd like to pick up my kids tonight."

"I can just as easily drop them off," Alison replied frostily. "No need to spoil their evening." Rage and hurt feelings battled for top position. How dare he think she had hustled this rich Texan and led him on, only to drop *him*, Blake! *He* was the one who had lied to her, not the other way around. She clenched her teeth and silently counted to ten as he stalked out the door.

"Dinner in ten minutes," she gritted out.

"Any more of that dandelion wine?" she heard Clem ask as she stormed into the kitchen.

Blake drove home, his hands clutching the wheel, his eyes staring straight ahead in an attempt to make some sense of the evening. As his temper slowly dissipated and things came into focus, he had to admit he'd acted rashly. But what was Alison trying to pull? Did she have a fetish for rich Texans? The thought of her angling after that oil-man made his blood boil. Was she trying to see who was richer? Tonight she'd walked out on him because he'd set up her interview with Carolina Webster. Maybe in the morning he could make sense of it. In the meantime he'd stock up on some groceries and return to wait for Sondra and Willy.

In the meantime, Clem had sobered up and gone back to his hotel, leaving Sally Jean snoring softly in the wing chair, oblivious to the blaring TV set and the squabble of Alison's three children. Marge had retired to her room to work on an astrology chart, and Alison had bundled Dog, Sondra and Willy into her station wagon. She'd done a lot of thinking and had to admit she had probably jumped to a few conclusions. Lord knew, Blake had! Maybe if they just sat down and talked they could come to an understanding. Anything was better than what she was going through now.

Sondra, who'd been quiet for most of the trip, suddenly said as they were turning into the driveway, "Thanks for everything, Alison. You know, I can tell that you and my dad have had a fight, but don't be too hard on him." She turned earnest eyes on Alison. "He really does mean well, and I know he likes you—a lot."

"That's strange advice coming from you, Sondra, but I'm glad you're feeling more open to your father."

"I probably wouldn't have if it hadn't been for you." She ran her gloved hands across the new handbag Alison had given her and said with a broad smile, "Let's go surprise my father!"

Dog began to bark excitedly in the back seat as Willy squirmed out the door. "Can he come, too?" he asked plaintively.

"I think he'll be better off here. I'll just be a minute."

"Bet Father asks you in for a drink." Sondra's voice was filled with confidence.

"Well, I do want to talk with him, but tomorrow would be better." Perhaps they could straighten things out then.

But, as the door swung open this hope was dashed to pieces, for greeting them—martini in hand—was the woman in the leopard coat.

Hot color leapt to Alison's face as she realized how quickly she had been replaced.

Chapter Eleven

A smile edged the woman's crimson mouth. Her teeth were large and brilliant like a model's and a very chic one at that. "I'll get Blake," she murmured in a sultry voice before disappearing.

Alison blinked back her disbelief. "Well, kids, your dad's home, so I'll just—"

"I don't know why *she's* back!" Sondra blurted out. "But you're not going to let her... let her just take my father, are you?"

"Aw, Sondra," Willy interjected, "the Leopard Lady was never a big deal."

"I don't like her." Sondra stared resolutely ahead of her, her mouth in a tight pout. Willy merely shrugged his shoulders and walked into the house.

"Tell your dad that I'll see him tomorrow," Alison said. She was trying to appear unruffled, but she knew she was failing miserably. Her voice wobbled, and if she wasn't careful she was liable to start crying. "Don't let Leopard

Lady get to you, honey.'' Impulsively she hugged Sondra and hurried down the path back to her car.

She drove through a blurry haze of tears, feeling as if her heart had been shattered into a million pieces and tossed to the four winds. At that moment she honestly didn't know how she was going to get through the night, much less tomorrow morning's interview. The image of a leopard coat and masses of blond hair rose up like a specter to haunt her. Alison slammed on her brakes as a light turned red, and, leaning against the steering wheel, she let out a sob. Dog leapt over the back seat and began to nudge her with his cold nose.

"Oh, Dog, Dog, what am I going to go?" She sniffed and lifted her head to look into chocolate eyes. Dog cocked his head in puzzlement and barked. "You're a big help," she said on a feeble laugh. Dog barked again, lunged forward and licked her face. "I know, I know, it's not the end of the world. It just feels like it."

The light changed and Alison turned onto Tulip Lane. Somehow she would survive this. She would go on with her life without Blake McLaughlin. Someday, looking back, she might even laugh at her folly. That first suspicious impression of him in New Orleans had been right. Why hadn't she listened to herself? He had never loved or needed her. What a fool she had been to have cloaked him in such glowing attributes.

The following morning threatened to be a glorious one. A hint of enamel blue slipped through the early pink dawn as Alison stared glumly out the kitchen window. With all this extra money that was flowing in she would hire a landscape gardener to bring some order to the riotous overgrowth known as the yard. Perhaps a psychiatrist could perform some similar feat with her brain and erase all memory of Blake McLaughlin and plant new seeds, though she doubted it.

The sun was rising faster now, a yellow ball perched above a cedar tree. Or was it a spruce? She thought of that morning when Blake had jogged alongside her at Monthaven Estate. He had said that Sondra had loved the place, and Alison had planned to take her back there. Feeling hot tears prick the back of her eyes, she took a shaky breath and tried to still them. It wouldn't do to appear bleary eyed on *Hello America.* Thankfully no one had come down to breakfast yet. Only Payowakit curled up on the windowsill, waiting for the sun. Days like this were as rare as a hen's teeth in Washington and normally Alison reveled in them, but not today.

There should be a law against such mornings, Alison thought as she poured a cup of coffee.

Blake was thinking similar thoughts as he let out an oath and dumped burned eggs into the sink.

"I wanted them sunny-side up, Dad," Willy complained as he reached into the cupboard for some cereal. Blake's hand lashed out, sending a shower of flakes to the floor.

"Gee, Dad, what'dya do that for?" Willy rescued the box of cereal and dumped some in a bowl.

"That's lousy breakfast food, that's why," Blake answered idiotically. Since when had he noticed which junk cereal his kids ate? He reached for a clean frying pan, butter and more eggs.

"Boy, what's burning?" Sondra asked as she appeared sleepy eyed and still in pink curlers.

"Dad's trying to cook," Willy informed her as he sloshed milk over his chocolate cereal. "So don't get in his way, he's in a bad mood." With a characteristic shrug of his shoulders, he headed for the table, crunching over spilled cereal. "I guess he's upset over last night." Seeing the warning look in Sondra's eyes, he quickly sat and applied himself to his breakfast.

"What do you mean 'upset over last night'?" Blake had successfully cracked three eggs and didn't dare take his eyes off them. When the only reply to his query was the clink of spoon against bowl, he asked, "What exactly did Alison tell you?"

"Nothing," Sondra replied a little too hastily. "Except that you felt it was time for us to come home, and that...that...she really liked you a lot!"

"Oh?" Blake swung around, spatula in hand. "She said all that?"

Sondra nodded eagerly. "She said that she'd never met anyone as nice as you." A hopeful smile touched her lips.

"Nice?" I've been called a lot of things, but 'nice'?" Behind him, the eggs began to sizzle. He didn't notice. "Well?"

"She did! She told us how much you meant to her, how she couldn't go on without you, how—"

"Aw, Sondra," Willy mumbled through a mouthful of cereal. "You sound like a soap opera."

"I do not!" she sniffed indignantly.

"I don't mind the TV patter, Sondra," Blake began softly. "I'm just surprised she said all that."

"Well, that was before the Leopard Lady answered the door." Sondra pursed her lips as if she'd bitten into something very bitter.

"You don't mean..." Blake, torn between the frying pan and Sondra's revelation, swiveled around once again.

"Yes, Father. Alison tried not to show her feelings, but I could tell she was upset."

"That's crazy," Blake sputtered.

"Why *was* Leopard Lady here, Dad?" Willy managed between mouthfuls of cereal.

"Trying, unsuccessfully I might add, to rekindle a dead fire!"

Sondra merely looked at him in wide-eyed wonder.

"It's true, dammit! She left right after you all arrived." He whirled back to the eggs and let out another, stronger, oath.

"Oh, well," Willy mumbled as he pushed away from the table, "Looks like we've got three real brown eggs!"

"Guess I'll go change," Sondra said sweetly.

Blake mouthed more obscenities as he dumped the second pan into the sink.

Ten minutes later Sondra reappeared. She had on a simple denim jumper over a light blue blouse. Her face, with only a hint of makeup, was somber, but the soft curls that framed it were quite pretty. Blake wanted to compliment his daughter, but the words wouldn't come.

It was Sondra who broke the silence, as in a matter-of-fact voice she said, "I'm surprised you'd go back to her, even if you and Alison *did* have a fight."

"I did not go back to her," Blake said in exasperation as he swung open the refrigerator door in search of non-existent eggs.

"There's raisin bread in the back," Sondra informed him. "I'll have that with peanut butter."

"Yuk!" Willy wrinkled his nose in distaste.

With a confident toss of her new hairdo, Sondra brushed past her brother, "It's better than the junk you eat!"

"That's enough, you two!" Blake slammed the bread onto the countertop. "I just want to get one thing straight with both of you. My relationship with Leopard Lady is nonexistent. She came here, and you all had the bad timing to—"

"To interrupt you and Leopard Lady," Willy supplied with a snicker.

"There was nothing to interrupt! The woman threw herself at me—"

"Where'd she go after she threw herself at you?" Sondra asked in a surprisingly adult tone as she spread peanut butter on her bread.

"Where do you think? Home! And if she's got good sense, she'll stay there." Blake ran a distracted hand through his hair as he yanked the refrigerator door open again, stared for a moment then slammed it.

"Well, something's eating you, and if it's not her it must be Alison." His daughter threw him a hopeful look before biting into her sandwich.

"I don't imagine it matters what Ms. Sherwood thinks of me." With an unsteady hand he poured hot water over instant coffee.

"Oh, but it does," Sondra managed in a peanut butter voice. She swallowed and continued, "She said she wanted to see you today, right after *Hello America*, and I don't think it was to talk sex shop." Sondra took a long drink of orange juice, eyed her father critically and said, "Dad, you shouldn't stand up when you're eating. Marge said—"

"I'm not eating," he snapped out. "I'm drinking coffee."

"That's bad for you, too."

"Valentino's is not a sex shop! And since when have you become a health expert?"

"Alison's mother has taught us a lot," Sondra said with satisfaction.

"Maybe she taught *you*," Willy corrected as he pushed his empty bowl from him and headed for the TV. "Time for Alison!"

"Oh, Dad's not interested in seeing *her*." Picking up the remains of her sandwich, she followed her younger brother into the living room.

"I didn't say that." Blake stood stock-still, feeling foolish and a little bested by his own kids. Maybe he should drop by the studio after the show. The TV station was only a few blocks away on Pennsylvania Avenue. At least he could clear up that ridiculousness concerning 'Leopard Lady.' Coffee in hand, he headed for the living room. . . .

" . . . And so, please welcome our first guest, Alison Sherwood, the vastly popular Georgetown designer who caught the eye of millionaire corporation president, Blake McLaughlin. Welcome, Ms. Sherwood."

"Oh, Lord," Blake muttered, practically spilling his coffee.

"Shh, Dad! Now we missed what Alison said." Sondra leaned forward and turned up the sound. Blake slumped down in his chair, one hand partially shading his eyes as if he had an impending headache.

"Knowing how people love a little gossip, please, could you put our minds to rest concerning the romance between you and your employer, Mr. McLaugh—"

"To begin with, he is not my employer, rather my client," Alison countered crisply.

"Oh, of course. Please excuse me." Carolina Webster gave a throaty laugh.

"And secondly, Mr. McLaughlin and I are business associates. There has certainly never been anything resembling a romance between us."

The interview continued as Blake sprang from his chair and strode to the door, a look of fury stamped on his face.

"Hey, Dad," Willy called out, "don't you want to see the rest of the show?"

"Keep watching that screen!" he replied over his shoulder as he stormed out the door.

"Oh, boy!" Sondra said, her gaze returning to the TV. "This should be interesting."

Alison felt like a fool. A very hot fool, at that, and the smile that was plastered on her overly made-up face was about to crack. Did they *have* to have those lights burning down on them like the noonday sun? Mad dogs and Englishmen go out in the noonday sun, she thought idiotically as Carolina Webster once again turned her crescent grin in Alison's direction. The commercial was over. It was time for more probing. Another ten minutes and it would be over.

Directly in front of Alison, Camera Two swiveled around and a young woman on the sidelines held up one finger. Just then a man with earphones scrambled onto the set and conferred in hushed tones with Carolina Webster. She smiled broadly, nodded and, leaning confidentially toward Alison, murmured, "Well! At the last minute he finally agreed." She turned toward the camera, poised and chic, and took a deep breath.

"We're fortunate indeed to have a special added attraction." She flicked her tongue over burgundy-colored lips and continued, "My second guest wasn't able to give me confirmation until the last minute, but I know you will give him a warm hand of applause." She flashed a Cheshire-cat smile into the camera and swiveled toward the side. "Ladies and gentlemen, Mr. Blake McLaughlin!"

Alison's throat felt as if a boulder were permanently lodged there. Blake was striding toward her with fierce determination and dark looks. Both the jacket and vest of his charcoal three-piece suit hung open, and the tie at his throat had obviously been knotted in haste. Abruptly he took a seat on the opposite side of Ms. Webster and perfunctorily shook her hand while his gaze caught and held Alison's.

"This is quite a coup for me," Carolina gushed in an attempt to claim Blake's attention. He flicked appraising eyes over her and she continued, "I've been trying for years to get Mr. McLaughlin on this show, and you'd think, when he bought the station, he'd acquiesce!" Her laughter climbed the scales, then quickly dropped to the throaty register that was her trademark. "Something tells me this is going to be quite a show." The look she fixed on Blake demanded a response.

He gave it.

"I didn't come here to chat," Blake began in a quiet and deadly voice, "but to try to knock some sense into this woman you're interviewing!" A choral gasp escaped the audience, followed by scattered applause and a few catcalls. Then a silence so intense Alison was sure everyone could hear her pulse thundering descended on the audience.

Carolina Webster managed a startled "My, my!" But Blake was oblivious to her and had eyes only for Alison.

"I love you!" he practically shouted. "And if you weren't so bullheaded, you'd have stuck around last night instead of slinking off." Alison opened her mouth to protest, but shock had stripped her vocal chords. Blake continued, "But I forgive you."

"*You* forgive me?" she managed to squeak out, unmindful of their rapt audience.

"I'm making an attempt to be funny and am probably making a fool of myself in the process, but since this is the only way I could get you to listen, and since it's impossible to get you alone—" he made a sweeping gesture to include cameras and audience "—I figured a million-or-so witnesses should suffice. That includes all of TV land. I also came to set the record straight. You and I most certainly shall have more going than a business relationship—"

"Blake, you can't just ... air these things in public!" Alison squirmed in her seat, then blurted out, "Think of your—my—reputation."

"To hell with our reputations. I'm in love with you and I want to marry you." He loosened his tie. "Now the whole world knows it. Well?"

"You're stark raving mad. You can't come in here and—" Alison looked to Carolina Webster, who had regained some of her composure, for assistance.

"Ms. Sherwood, he *owns* WNBR!" She shrugged, fastened her cool gray eyes on the raving madman and said to Alison, "You're the envy of every female viewer, and I must say I'd be rather impressed if my man declared himself in front of millions of people."

"But this is ridiculous." Turning her attention back to Blake, she added, "For someone who claimed it was difficult to express himself, you certainly are—"

"Blathering like an idiot with no tomorrow. Want to call the funny farm? It's true I finagled this interview, but only as a way to thank you for what you did for Sondra."

"But you should have told me!" Alison protested, ignoring Carolina Webster's bobbing head as she followed the verbal tennis match.

"You know you wouldn't have agreed to appear here if I told you. But dammit, Alison, you're talented and you deserve a break."

"I was doing very nicely—"

"I know, I know!" Running a hand through his hair, Blake slowed the pace. "I know you didn't really need help. It was just my way of thanking you. And you know how hard it is for me to put feelings into words.''

"You're certainly making up for lost time," Alison said softly.

"I'm trying, because if I lose you, I lose everything. I want to marry you! What more can I say?"

"Marry the poor sucker!" someone in the front row shouted.

"Yeah, marry him!" someone else yelled. Suddenly the entire audience was shouting "Marry him, marry him!" and "He loves you!" Blake grinned and waved to the now-cheering crowd that had risen to their feet.

"Kinda like being an opera star in the Met. Wanna take a bow?"

"Oh, Blake, this is madness." Alison looked out at the sea of faces and back to Blake. "What do we do now?" she cried out.

"Oh, for heaven's sake, kiss and make up!" Carolina said. She directed an unruffled smile at the camera and added, "We'll be right back after these messages. Don't go away."

"Blake, I can't think here." Alison pressed her hands over her ears. The audience, thoroughly enjoying this early-morning drama, was now clapping, stomping and chanting in unison, "Marry him! Marry him!"

"How much time do we have?" Blake casually asked Carolina, "Two minutes?"

"Something like that," she replied on a feigned yawn.

"I don't think they're going to stop until you say you'll marry me, Alison."

"This is blackmail," she sputtered. "I came here to talk about my business, not about my love life!"

"Marry me," he whispered, rising and crossing to her chair.

"I'm...I'm confused. I've never been good in crowds." Tears were pricking her eyes and a wave of heat branded her face.

"Trust me." He drew her to her feet.

The audience's cheers crescendoed and Carolina Webster said, "Welcome back. As you can see, some progress had been made."

"Blake, this is—"

"Madness," he murmured as his lips neared hers. "Now, for the last time, will you marry me? What d'ye say, Cotton Candi?"

"Yes." Tears sprung to her eyes and streamed down her face. "Yes, you crazy madman. Anything to stop them." She made a vague gesture to the wildly clapping audience, and that seemed to silence them.

Blake laughed, "You're a powerful woman. You have them eating out of the palm of your hand." Gently he tilted her face toward his. "Now, say you'll marry me because you love me."

Alison tried to swallow the lump in her throat. He really loved her and he let the world know it. Her voice, low and ragged, murmured, "Yes, of course, I'll marry you, because I do love you so very much." She saw her love reflected in the dancing light of his eyes as he pulled her closer. Their hearts were beating as one now, and it sent a thrill of rapture coursing through her.

As his mouth closed over hers in a long and achingly tender kiss, the audience once again burst into a rousing applause.

Epilogue

"And to think all this time I've been calling you my little Eskimo," Blake teased as he propped himself up on one elbow and stared at his wife of two weeks. "And," he added, leaning over to lather more suntan lotion on her back, "you're the most peculiar Irishwoman I've known. You tan."

She slanted him a languorous look. "And just how many colleens have you known?"

"None so luscious as you." His hand slipped down her bare back, inched beneath the white suit and pinched her soft, round bottom. Playfully she slapped his hand. Rolling onto her side, she let out a long sigh and smiled up at him. It was almost sunset, and on his little Caribbean island that she'd never heard of before, nightfall dropped like a curtain on a spectacular three-act play. She breathed deeply of the salty air and reveled in the feel of tropical breezes that ruffled her sun-warmed body.

"We should come here often," Alison said lazily as her fingers drummed a tattoo on Blake's tanned chest.

"You have a willing travel partner. I am of the firm belief that all work and no play does make for a dull boy."

"There's nothing dull about you, honey," she whispered, nestling closer to him. His merest touch sent pleasure rippling through her, enlivening her senses and sparking a desire that consumed them both. Perhaps it was the warmth of the tropical sun or the delicious food or something in the water, but she had never experienced such ecstasy with a man. She joked about him being custommade for her, but it was true. She had never thought to find a man as wonderful as Blake McLaughlin.

"Let's stay another week," he whispered in her ear as he traced a fiery path down her back.

"I suppose I could call work." Her reply was muffled against his mouth. Softly he plundered it, his tongue flicking in and out like a flame—hot and full of promise and desire. Slowly she withdrew from him and, pulling herself to a sitting position, eased one spaghetti strap off her nut-brown shoulder. She smiled at his intake of breath as the top slipped lower. He reached toward her, but with a wicked smile she evaded him.

"Do you like to look?" she asked in her most sultry voice as she slipped off the other strap. Slowly she began to unfasten the cross laces that held the suit together.

"This is torture, and I love it." In a swift motion he lunged for her. "Got you!"

She laughed and rolled away from him. Coming to a kneeling position, she pulled the pins from her dark hair and let it tumble around her shoulders. They hadn't made love on the beach since that first night, and she'd been reluctant when he suggested it. Until she learned that Blake owned the island! A seawall surrounded the ivory crescent of beach that was a stone's throw from their hideaway—a ten-room Spanish-style hacienda complete with courtyard, tinkling fountains, swimming pool and sauna! Blake jokingly called it their Caribbean cottage.

"Would you like a swim?" Alison suggested meaningfully.

"Later." This time when he reached for her, she melted into his arms, succumbing to the shiver of desire that spilled over her, vibrating every fiber of her being. Boldly she drew her hands down the flat plane of his stomach. It was warm and hard and full of desire. She thrilled to his touch as it followed a similar path on her eager body. Down, down his fingers went, skillfully caressing her silken skin. Gradually, ever so gradually, he stirred the liquid flame until she felt every inch of her fill with a desire that demanded satisfaction. This gossamer chord of ecstasy was sending them higher and higher into their own private galaxy.

"Oh, Blake," she murmured, arching her body toward him. The sand was a soft cushion beneath them, yet she was only aware of the growing need that left her breathless and yearning for more.

"Yes, yes, my darling." His voice was full of husky longing as he pressed himself against her.

In the distance the soft lapping of timeless shore washed upon white sands and the trade winds whispered their secrets to the swaying palm trees.

At length Blake whispered, "I think we'll need to stay another week."

"You're the captain," Alison replied on a sigh of pleasure that was caught on a sea breeze and carried away.

* * *

"Listen to this," Alison said over breakfast their first morning back. "It's a letter from my sister, Sarah. You remember her, she came up for the wedding."

"I'm forever indebted to her for bringing us together! And for taking care of the kids while we were on our honeymoon."

"Well, she, Mom and the kids will be flying into Dulles from New Orleans in the morning." Alison continued scanning the letter. "Oh, and she says Robin wants us to buy a big house with an iron balcony like they have in New Orleans, and it must have a swimming pool!" Absently Alison stirred her coffee. "I don't know about the swimming pool, but it will be nice moving into a brand-new space."

"With a swimming pool," Blake commented as he bit off the corner of a croissant and waved the remains at Alison. "Marge won't approve of this rich fare, you know."

Alison laughed, "I think she'll continue to overlook your minor vices. Oh, listen to this. Sally Jean and her oilman dropped by on their way to Corpus Christi. Seems she's back up to size sixteen, but Clem loves her that way. And there's more!" Alison took a bracing gulp of lukewarm coffee. "Hannah is coming back!"

"Hannah? Is that one of your children I haven't met or another pet?"

"Our old domestic!" Reading from the letter, Alison continued, "'Hannah says she's decided to forego her past life as a silent-screen star and come back to Washington, D.C., where people are sane.' Ha!" Finishing off her coffee, she stood abruptly. "Okay, my handsome, virile lover of a husband, let's go look at this shack you want us to buy, that is, unless you're up for a little more early-morning exercise." She winked knowingly and dashed from the table, Dog and Blake in hot pursuit.

"Why the big rush?" he called after her, grabbing their coats from the rack by the front door.

"Because you ignorant man, you, Marge says we have to do it before Mercury goes retrograde, and also the moon goes void—of course—at noon!" She paused and bit back a grin. "I warned you life with the O'Shaunnessey-Sherwoods would be a madcap adventure, but you *would* make that TV appearance."

"Well, what do you think?"

"I feel like Scarlett O'Hara. Isn't it a bit big?" Her voice echoed in the high-ceilinged room.

"No way, sweet thing, and I think you'll particularly like this." He opened a paneled door leading into a small boudoir off the master bedroom. A shiny red satin swing in a mirrored room greeted them.

"Blake! What will people think when they see it?" On an intake of breath she whirled to face him. "Why, you've already bought the place!"

"Yes, and to answer your question, no one will see it." He drew her into his arms on a long chuckle.

"You really are the most—"

He silenced her mock protestations with a very satisfying kiss before releasing her. "Infuriating man you've ever met. Ah, but wait till you see the pink flamingo by the pool."

"Blake." Her warning note turned to laughter and, throwing her arms around him, she murmured, "You're the most wonderful man a woman could have, and I'm about the luckiest woman alive."

He smiled his wonderful smile. "Don't you want to try out your swing, Cotton Candi?"

* * * * *

Silhouette Classics

COMING IN APRIL...

THORNE'S WAY by Joan Hohl

When *Thorne's Way* first burst upon the romance scene in 1982, readers couldn't help but fall in love with Jonas Thorne, a man of bewildering arrogance and stunning tenderness. This book quickly became one of Silhouette's most sought-after early titles.

Now, Silhouette Classics is pleased to present the reissue of *Thorne's Way*. Even if you read this book years ago, its depth of emotion and passion will stir your heart again and again.

And that's not all!

Silhouette Special Edition

COMING IN JULY...

THORNE'S WIFE by Joan Hohl

We're pleased to announce a truly unique event at Silhouette. Jonas Thorne is back, in *Thorne's Wife*, a sequel that will sweep you off your feet! Jonas and Valerie's story continues as life—and love—reach heights never before dreamed of.

Experience both these timeless classics—one from Silhouette Classics and one from Silhouette Special Edition—as master storyteller Joan Hohl weaves two passionate, dramatic tales of everlasting love!

NAVY BLUES
Debbie Macomber

Between the devil and the deep blue sea...

At Christmastime, Lieutenant Commander Steve Kyle finds his heart anchored by the past, so he vows to give his ex-wife wide berth. But Carol Kyle is quaffing milk and knitting tiny pastel blankets with a vengeance. She's determined to have a baby, and only one man will do as father-to-be—the only man she's ever loved...her own bullheaded ex-husband!

You met Steve and Carol in NAVY WIFE (Special Edition #494)—you'll cheer for them in NAVY BLUES (Special Edition #518). (And as a bonus for NAVY WIFE fans, newlyweds Rush and Lindy Callaghan reveal a surprise of their own....)

Each book stands alone—together they're Debbie Macomber's most delightful duo to date! Don't miss

NAVY BLUES
Available in April,
only in *Silhouette Special Edition*.
Having the "blues" was never
so much fun!

Silhouette Intimate Moments®

Let Bestselling Author KATHLEEN EAGLE Sweep You Away to De Colores Once Again

For the third time, Kathleen Eagle has written a book set on the spellbinding isle of De Colores. In PAINTBOX MORNING (Intimate Moments #284), Miguel Hidalgo is all that stands between his island home and destruction—and Ronnie Harper is the only woman who can help Miguel fulfill his destiny and lead his people into a bright tomorrow. But Ronnie has a woman's heart, a woman's needs. In helping Miguel to live out his dreams, is she destined to see her own dreams of love with this very special man go forever unfulfilled? Read PAINTBOX MORNING, coming this month from Silhouette Intimate Moments, and follow the path of these star-crossed lovers as they build a future filled with hope and a love to last all time.

If you like PAINTBOX MORNING, you might also like Kathleen Eagle's two previous tales of De Colores: CANDLES IN THE NIGHT (Special Edition #437) and MORE THAN A MIRACLE (Intimate Moments #242).
